Goddess Bedtime Stories

21 Tales to Keep You Up All Night
Edited by Jennifer Jolicoeur

Athena's Home Novelties
640 Winter Street
Woonsocket, RI 02895

ISBN: 978-0-9831806-0-9

Library of Congress Control Number: 2010918142

Printed in the United States of America on acid-free paper.

This book is dedicated to Goddesses everywhere –
and the lovers who adore them.

Table of Contents

Part One: Choose Your Own Adventure

I've Been Everywhere   3
By Mother Goddess Jennifer Jolicoeur

One Spring Night   15
By Goddess Laurie Picot

Breaking My Own Rules   21
By Goddess Angel Maldonado Lopez

Element of Surprise   27
By Goddess Sherry Harmon

The Orthopedist's Wife   33
By Goddess Angela Goldsberry

Part Two: Mystery

Mystery Girl   43
By Goddess Molly Whitman

Pancakes   47
By Goddess Carmen dePina

Lavender Diamond   53
By Goddess Barbara Rutenkroger

The Stranger   59
By Goddess Alicia Orlow

Part Three: Playing At Work

Salon Sexcapades   65
By Goddess Monica Holbrook

Joe's   71
By Goddess Karen Horn

Day After Day   79
By Goddess Rachael Laurie

The Ideal Retail Experience   85
By Goddess Jamie Winchester

Part Four: Romance

Waking and Wanting   93
By Goddess Corinne Geary

Who Says You Can't Go Home Again   99
By Goddess Jan Simard

Picture Perfect   **107**
By Goddess Jennifer Wilson

Le Petit Mort   **115**
By Goddess Christine Laplante

Part Five: Graphic Novel

Giggles   **123**
By Goddess Mary Brown

Chinese Food   **131**
By Goddess Amanda Burden

All The Discomforts of Home   **139**
By Goddess Maggie Russell

Lipstick   **143**
By Goddess Christine Reid

About Athena's Home Novelties   **151**

Featured Products   **153**

Acknowledgments

A few years ago, my dear friend and super star Athena's Goddess, Regena Garrepy, gave me a necklace that held a shiny golden sphere with a tiny scroll inside. The enclosed card instructed me to write my dream on the scroll and place it inside the orb. Yet I found the teeny, tiny scroll too small to write on, especially given that I am blessed to have a mother who always encouraged my dreams. Therefore, I have hundreds of them still yet to manifest. How do I pick just one, I wondered.

I resolved to choose a very important dream; one I knew would make my mom proud. I picked up a purple pen—because I feel more whimsical and creative when I write in purple ink—and wrote: "Publish a book before I am 40."

I then rolled up this little scroll and placed it inside the orb. When I slipped it over my head, the orb landed in the center of my chest. Thank you, Regena. You set the birth of this book in motion by pressing my dream against my heart.

Thank you, Mom, for never holding me back and cheering me on every day of my life. When I hear my inner voice of hope, it's your voice I hear.

I've learned that I must surround myself with other big dreamers in this world.

To my mentors Marcia Weider, America's Dream Coach, and Jack Canfield, America's Success Coach—you both inspire me daily.

To Caterina Rando the gorgeous, passionate speaker and author—thank you for sharing your wisdom when I needed it most. I'm glad I shared my dream with you.

Thank you to everyone who submitted stories. I am so grateful to you for sharing your talents. You answered my call. It was a pleasure to read every single story.

Thanks to my judges—I know it was tough to choose just twenty—and we all powered through!

To Lauren and Herschel from Green Imaging, maybe one day this book will become our first erotic film. That would be a fun shoot!

Debra Cotnoir—In a world of day-to-day troubleshooting, I figured this would be a fun project to master (way more fun than sales taxes).

To my sister-in-law and dear friend, Robyn Jolicoeur—thank you for being a judge. I can always count on you.

To my life long best friends, Michelle "Berardski" Berard and Jason Fortin—I so appreciate your love and support.

Thank you to our gorgeous cover model, Goddess #629 Amy Bishop! Your arse is famous now, but I treasure every part of you! Photographer Leah Stafford snapped this shot during a boudoir photo session. I appreciate her keen eye.

Mike Balint and Dawn Bagley at MIBA Design have been making Athena's look beautiful for a decade. As they always do, they have brought my vision to life. Mike, you are so thorough and passionate about your design work. Everything you do is infused with integrity. I thank the Goddess for you every day.

To my dream team and soul sisters at Athena's—thank you for supporting my dreams and believing in me!

To Pepere Normand—thanks for the open and honest conversations about sex that we've shared. You are my hero.

To Mr. Menard, my fourth grade teacher—it is because of you that I write.

To all the good people over at THRIVE Publishing™—thank you for proofing and guiding me through the process of creating this book. This is the first, and it won't be the last time we work together!

And finally—to my husband, lover and friend, Curtis Jolicoeur. You've been making me tingle all over since I was just a girl. Marrying you was the best thing I ever manifested!

Goddess Bless,

Jennifer Jolicoeur

Foreword

In early 2009, I challenged the men and women who make Athena's the best adult toy company on the planet to write and submit an erotic story for this book. Entries arrived as fast as a quickie in the shower!

Next came the titillating task of reading all the stories and choosing only 20, plus my own, of course.

My husband Curtis and I lost ourselves in a sea of erotic tales. We spent days reading and discussing what elements and scenarios were most arousing. Staying on task was challenging. There was a reoccurring need to relieve the pressure of erotica overload.

My team of judges had similar experiences—becoming hot and bothered over and over for days on end. How fortunate for us all! (I'll be upfront with you now and state that the side effects of this book include increased communication and great sex. Consult your Goddess for more details!)

What I appreciated most was how these tales transported me into an adventurous, spontaneous and passionate state of being.

Wouldn't you agree that those are three key ingredients for a healthy, happy and mutually rewarding sex life? After more than 15 years of sex with the same partner, I am certain they are.

I also believe that sexual fantasy makes for hotter, wetter and better sex.

Since childhood, I've been a fantasy girl, tenaciously tapping into the deep and rich well of my imagination. There has always been a plethora of people, places and possibilities dancing vibrantly in my mind. This still serves me well in the sanctuary that is my bedroom.

When I fantasize during sex, it's not that I wish I was with someone other than my gifted and generous lover. I wouldn't trade Curtis for any one (including a young David Gilmour). Yet my mind is filled with uninhibited sexual scenarios. Compiling these stories proved I'm not the only one. The nineteen women and one man who contributed to this book are brave and compelled to share those fantasies that bring on the most explosive of orgasms—all for your pleasure.

I love this because we're all entitled to and deserve more pleasure.

Through Athena's home parties, I've met thousands of women who struggle to embrace their perfectly normal and natural sexual desires. Women have complained to me for more than a decade about unsatisfying sex lives with partners who work too much or overindulge in television or the Internet until their brains, bodies and libidos turn to mush.

Our culture consistently bears witness to baffling celebrity infidelity. What kind of a fool cheats on gorgeous stars like Halle Berry, Christie Brinkley and Sandra Bullock? Even the Gores are getting divorced. So I ask myself: Where are the satisfied lovers? Where are the people who are setting off sexual fireworks when they touch each other?

Obviously, there need to be more champions for extraordinary sex in this world. I'm one of them. It is my hope that this book will help lovers deepen their desire to communicate and play. I hold the vision that women especially will connect with a sensual part of themselves again—or for the first time.

My intention is that you, the reader, relax in a tub or sacred space with this book. Find your favorite story: the one that forces you to put the book down because you are having trouble balancing it while you touch yourself! If you want more information about the products mentioned in some of the stories, see pages 153-159 at the back of this book.

Arousal like this is too good to keep to yourself. This book is meant to be shared. Perch yourself on the edge of your bed and seductively offer to read a bedtime story to your special someone.

Trust me. He or she will be intrigued.

It is my ultimate wish that you will read this book and stay up all night having the best sex of your life!

Goddess Bless,

Jennifer Jolicoeur

Part One

Choose Your Own Adventure

How liberating to lie back and imagine yourself as a daring sexual being, willing to take charge to ensure you achieve your desired (ahem) "outcome."

I've Been Everywhere By Mother Goddess Jennifer Jolicoeur   3

One Spring Night By Goddess Laurie Picot   15

Breaking My Own Rules By Adonis Angel Maldonado Lopez   21

Element of Surprise By Goddess Sherry Harmon   27

The Orthopedist's Wife By Goddess Angela Goldsberry   33

I've Been Everywhere

By Mother Goddess Jennifer Jolicoeur

My business travels take me around the globe. I've spent more time in airports, hotel rooms and business meetings than I care to mention.

There is no space in my life to care for a potted plant, never mind a needy lover, so I never leave home without my trusty Celebrator®. I bought it at an Athena's Home Novelties party my sister organized the last time I was home. It's like the Tupperware® parties my mom held when I was a kid. Only this party had fun gadgets for the bedroom, not the kitchen.

The sex toy lady called herself a Goddess. I liked that. During her very entertaining presentation, she made it sound like the Celebrator was the "must have" for every woman. Her claim was that it made the female orgasm more intense in sensation and longer in duration.

"I'll take it," I proclaimed out loud, much to my sister's embarrassment.

I have to tell you, it was the very best $50 investment I've ever made. The deep down body pleasure is akin to eating a Godiva® truffle while getting a foot massage by Johnny Depp on a tropical beach! Many interesting fantasies have surfaced while using it to bring on those undeniably long and intense orgasms. My mind tends to conjure up all kinds of sexual scenarios whenever the Celebrator touches my clit. I take it everywhere, and it returns the favor by taking me places I've never been—and I've been everywhere.

This story is not about my Celebrator, however, but more about the night in Orlando when it broke.

There I was in Room 1312 at the Hyatt, laying naked on the crisp white sheets with the last of the day's sunlight filtering in through the window. My mind was exploring the possibilities of a multiple partner fantasy.

The Celebrator and I were on our way to yet another climax when all of a sudden, it stopped working. Panic set in. I spent thirty minutes fiddling with the battery connectors in a whole-hearted attempt to fix it. I even dressed and went down to the gift shop where I spent $12.00 for two new AA batteries. No dice.

It was then that a deep sadness washed over me. The Celebrator and I had traveled the world together these last 18 months. And now it was over.

I pressed it to my breast, on the verge of tears, mourning the fact I would have to deposit it in the trashcan and leave it behind. Then, two things occurred to me. I needed to buy two next time; I would never leave home without a back-up again. More importantly, I was confronted with the fact that I had not had sex with a human being in almost two years.

Me.

No real sex.

For two years.

In that sad moment, an aching from the center of my body overpowered me. My pussy was angry, unfulfilled and demanding release. I'm sure I could have used my fingers, but that just wasn't going to do it. It would be like going to McDonald's® in an evening gown. My clitoris had become accustomed to high velocity stimulation.

I contemplated my options as I teetered on the edge of frustration still clutching my now dear departed Celebrator.

I flipped open my Mac® laptop and basked in its gentle glow before typing three words into the search engine that would take me somewhere I had never been: Orlando Swingers Club.

Gosh, I just love the Internet. In seconds, I had all the information I needed to walk straight into my fantasy and satisfy the demands of my still wet and wanting pussy.

After a quick shower, I primped and preened before the mirror. Long red curls hung around my face, cascaded down my shoulders and tickled the center of my back. My large, round breasts looked magnificent with blush nipples standing at attention. The neatly manicured hair on my pubic mound covered my juicy swollen lips. This body of mine was ready for a human touch.

Next, I found myself stepping out of a yellow cab in front of a huge purple home with a green door. Above it, a wooden sign read: Dew Drop Inn. The Florida heat swallowed me whole. I glanced up and down the street. I noticed how the other large homes looked the same, with picket fences out front and telephone poles covered with masses of tangled ivy lining the street. I wondered if the neighbors knew what went on at the Inn. I handed the cab driver $18. Did he know where he had taken me? He wished me a pleasant evening and sped away into the sticky night.

With confidence and no reservations, I climbed the stairs and rang the doorbell.

As I waited, I realized I was not surprised I had come this far. I had acted swiftly and deliberately. No fear. No regrets. In all aspects of my life, I take risks and get what I want. A seat upgrade, the table by the window, the biggest clients my industry has to offer, and tonight I was ready to get exactly what I wanted sexually. A shiver of anticipation danced down my spine.

The door swung open to reveal a petite brunette with the biggest brown eyes I'd ever seen. From behind her, a blast of air conditioning tickled my skin. I found it odd that she was wearing a stewardess outfit. Her breasts bulged out of her low-cut navy blue dress. The red ascot tied around her throat was the perfect contrast to her alabaster skin.

"Welcome to the Dew Drop Inn. This is where your fantasies take flight." she said, motioning behind her and grinning. "Welcome aboard. I'm Kinky Freedman."

She turned, and I followed her. She was lovely—like Betty Boop in white fishnets and red stilettos.

"What brings you here tonight?" she asked, without looking back at me.

"I broke my favorite sex toy about two hours ago at a crucial moment," I answered.

She spun around giggling. "Are you serious?"

"Yes." I took a step closer to her. She smelled like candy.

"Well, I assure you that you've come to the right place to finish what you started," she said coyly.

"Are you always dressed like a flight attendant?" I inquired.

"No. It's the theme for tonight," she said, running her palms down the front of her dress.

"I wish I had known."

"Don't you worry your pretty head. We need travelers too."

We had made our way down the hall to a softly lit open area decorated with elaborate draperies and lavish throw pillows. Kama Sutra artwork adorned the walls and nude sculptures stood in every corner. It was as though I had been transported to another world. Just three minutes before I had been in a musty cab. But that was in the past. I had to stay present and focused on the many possibilities the immediate future held for me.

I walked into quite a scene. My eyes scanned the room. A couple locked in an embrace on a velvet settee were rocking back and forth slowly, the man fingering the woman gently under her skirt. On the oversized couch, four people huddled in secret conversation. On the loveseat closest to me, two women sat beside a muscular gentleman, like blond bookends, one touching the buttons of his shirt, the other sliding her hand up and down his thigh.

"This is the central meeting point," Kinky said, sweeping the air with her arm. "Rendezvous take place in rooms that line the hall through that doorway." She motioned with both hands as though they were the emergency exit rows.

I leaned in to her and whispered. "I've never flown before. Could you give me a little guidance?"

She stayed in character. "I'd be happy to take you to the flight deck and introduce you to our captain and his co-pilot. They happen to be brothers, who know their way around the cockpit."

I followed Kinky through the French doors on the other side of the meeting room, our high heels clicking in time on the shiny hardwood floor. She stopped and knocked on a mahogany door.

"Come in," called a husky voice.

Kinky led the way into the large bedroom. There stood two gorgeous men—tall and lean. One dressed in navy blue pants with a white button-down shirt. His sandy blond bangs hung just over his eyebrows. The other was dressed exactly the same but with shorter hair. Each had eyes the color of emeralds. They were obviously brothers as Kinky had mentioned minutes before, and after closer examination, I realized they were twins. Each sported a pin shaped like an airplane above their shirt pocket.

It's funny how much a plane looks like a dildo with wings, I thought.

They smiled and stepped forward to greet Kinky with a kiss on the cheek before turning their eyes to me. Kinky introduced us.

"This is Curtis and Joel. They are the proprietors of the Dew Drop Inn." And with that she realized she hadn't even asked my name.

"I'm Anne." I smiled, thrusting my hand forward. It's what I do in business—and I was planning on doing business tonight.

"How do you do," said Curtis. His voice was deep.

"Pleased to meet you, Anne," said Joel, as he turned my wrist and brought my hand to his full lips. I couldn't recall a time when a man kissed my hand upon meeting me.

Although I was swooning, I noticed that they both had big hands.

"This is Anne's first time flying," Kinky explained. "I'm sure you gentleman can give her a smooth ride."

She reached for the door, and I reached for her hand. I didn't want her to go.

"I'd love it if you could stay, Kinky."

We locked eyes.

She motioned to Curtis and Joel for approval; they shrugged.

"I'd love to," she beamed.

Curtis sat down on the edge of the bed. "Where would you like to go tonight, Anne?" he asked.

Moans filtered in from the room next door. Joel smiled secretly.

I moved towards the bed and took a seat next to Curtis; our shoulders touched. Joel followed me to the bed and sat on the other side of me. I was quite pleased to find myself in the middle of a beefcake sandwich. So far, so good.

"It's your journey," Kinky purred, while simultaneously dropping her dress. Her matching red and white polka dotted bra and panties covered the mysteries of her body I now desperately wanted to uncover.

They were awaiting my response while I searched my mind for some aeronautical comeback.

"I like to fly first class."

"We always board our first class passengers before anyone else," Curtis purred in my ear.

He pushed me down on to my back while Joel made quick work of the buttons down the front of my dress. Kinky's greedy hands were already tugging at my panties.

Curtis pulled the fabric of my bra to the side and took one nipple into his mouth while Joel did the same. I felt a rush of euphoria I had never known as they sucked, nibbled and licked.

Kinky was spreading my pussy wide open. She pulled my lips back tightly exposing my clit. She pushed her wet tongue into my hungry hole and wiggled it furiously. As the focus of this holy trinity, I surrendered completely.

Kinky was drinking me, lapping in long strokes careful not to touch my swollen clit just yet.

Curtis abandoned my nipple to kiss my lips. His tongue explored my mouth while Kinky did the same to my pussy. He was delicious and tender. Joel was still sucking my nipple, cupping the other breast in his hand and then rolling my damp nipple with his thumb and forefinger. At my mouth, Curtis abruptly replaced his tongue with his rigid cock.

He lifted the back of my head, angling me for deeper penetration. His other hand stroked my stomach, his fingers reaching down to grab my pussy lips—seizing them from Kinky. With two strong fingers he held me open for Kinky, pulling me open even wider still.

Joel remained at my nipples. He sucked and twisted and twisted and sucked.

I opened my throat to Curtis inviting him deeper, caressing the underside of his meaty shaft. And after what felt like eternity, Kinky finally darted her tongue around my clit. While her nails grazed my thighs, she devoured me. After a burst of firm and deliberate lapping, she enveloped my clit with her soft lips, drawing more of my hypersensitive flesh into her mouth; all the while, her tongue glided like silk across the nerve center.

My mind was melting with sensory overload. Where to focus? Energy zipped around my body like an electrical current.

I was moaning into Curtis' cock, unable to scream at the onset of my orgasm. The only sound that could escape was a whimper that made its way around his slippery dick. This seemed to impress him for he thrusted faster, pulling my hair, but not too hard—just enough to bring my attention to the sensation of his fingers and palm on my head.

Kinky slipped two fingers into me and pulled forward. Oh, the pressure! The sweet pressure building. And there I lingered, on the edge, right where I was when my sweet Celebrator died just hours before. This time, I was not fantasizing.

It was in that glorious space between beginning and end that rapture did come. I could swear that my body lifted off the bed. My fists beat the soft fabric of the bedspread. I was not alone. Curtis erupted, filling my throat in a warm and wonderful series of spasms. When he withdrew his pulsing penis, my muffled squeals were free to emerge. I gasped and then cried out. Curtis released my pussy lips. Kinky's tongue moved back down to my slit and licked my cum. With a satisfied "mmmmm", she pulled her fingers out slowly. There was heat and then there was emptiness.

Kinky moved away from me, and Joel mounted me. Curtis and Kinky each held a leg back while Joel pushed his dick into me. There is no greater joy than getting fucked after an oral explosion. I felt so ready to receive him.

With feline stealth, Kinky moved her body over me, dropping her candy-scented pussy just inches above my mouth. She was shaved smooth and so tasty. My tongue found her groove easily, and she rocked back and forth purring. The harder Joel fucked me, the faster I licked Kinky. I held her thighs and pressed the pads of my fingertips into her flesh. When her clit began to pulse, I felt her body rise, trying to flee. Her cries of pleasure becoming louder. I held her tight and lifted my head to stay with her, to taste her juicy orgasm.

Kinky collapsed, panting, and fell sideways beside me on to the bed. Curtis dropped my leg and moved to her. He flipped her over on her belly and pulled her hips to him. He was ready for round two. I watched her tits sway back and forth as he pumped her.

"You. Like. Watching. Her. Get. Fucked. Don't. You?" Joel growled into my ear. Each word punctuated with a deep thrust.

I could only whimper a response.

He fucked me harder—relentlessly—until my pussy began to quake. I felt my own slippery liquid gush all over him.

With that he was gone, moving his gorgeous body in front of Kinky, whose mouth was perfect for fucking. I rolled over on my side to watch the way the brothers penetrated her, one in front and the other from behind. They moved with perfect precision as the masters of her pleasure. Beads of sweat flew as they erupted one by one and landed breathless on their backs.

I was completely electrified with the sexual energy of these three beings. The intensity of it made it's way through every inch of my body.

"Thank you," I said. "I had a most pleasant flight."

One Spring Night

By Goddess Laurie Picot

It was a warm April Night, warmer than usual for Boston this time of year. I was out enjoying the summer-like feel that was a nice change from the cold and rainy days we'd been having when I felt my phone vibrating in my pocket. I was half expecting to hear from him since it had been a while since I had last fucked him.

He sounded like a thirteen-year-old boy that just got caught by his Mom with a Playboy® magazine under his bed. He nervously asked if I had any plans for the evening and I knew we were going to have some fun. When I said I didn't, he blurted out his invitation: would I be interested in having a threesome with him and his girlfriend? He explained this was something they had been talking about for a while and she finally decided she wanted to do it. It was her first time and she was a little shy. He immediately thought of me because he knew that I'd be perfect for their first experience.

I didn't even have to think about it. Of course I would. It had been a while since I had last been with a woman and the chance to be her first was something that I could not turn down. Plus, I had fond memories of his thick cock.

I told Jason I could be there in an hour. He sounded giddy as he fumbled over the address, reminding me of a kid in a candy store.

"Okay, okay, so we will see you soon?"

I laughed and assured him I would be there before they knew it.

As I was putting myself together, figuring out what to wear, my excitement started to rise. I was definitely getting wet, but was I getting nervous too? Could be, but that was half the fun. There is something so erotic and taboo about being part of a threesome—and I would be the experienced one, the one in control.

I chose my outfit carefully, even though I knew if things went according to plan, it wouldn't be on very long. I decided that a low-cut white blouse and short plaid skirt with my three inch heels would do the trick. I wore a lacy white bra underneath that barely covered my nipples and a matching thong that was already drenched by the time I got out to the car.

I pulled up in front of her house just over an hour after his phone call. Making them wait was half the fun, the anticipation of it all. I checked my makeup for the last time as I locked my car and made my way to her door. I took one last deep breath and rang the doorbell. Jason answered wearing nothing but his boxer shorts and God did he look great. He had unruly dark brown hair and blue eyes that always looked like they were up to something. His chest was bare and muscular, but those arms! Those arms always do it for me. They have the perfect amount of definition and I just love grabbing hold of them while riding that nice hard cock of his. But not tonight—tonight was all about her.

He didn't say much as he led me into the candlelit living room. I think he was too worked up and aroused to make a full sentence. I could see his cock thickening through the thin layer of his boxers.

They had put a lot of planning into tonight. There were carefully placed candles that danced around the room, and they had pushed together two backless pieces of the couch to make a massage table. She was laying on top of it, already naked, her skin glistening from the massage oil in the candlelight. She had the most perfect curves and an ass you could take a bite out of.

As he was fumbling with the massage oil, he asked if I would like to join. Without a word, I removed my clothes. After all, I didn't want to be the only one dressed. I let Jason put some massage oil on my hands and started on the back of her calves as he worked on her back. As I was massaging her, I was able to study her more. She was so very beautiful, with perfect tan legs that led up to a gorgeous ass. She had a tribal tattoo in the small of her back and long blond hair that half covered her face.

As we massaged her together she let out a soft moan here and there. She was completely relaxed. I took it slow; I didn't want to seem too eager. I carefully moved up her legs not missing a spot, from her calves to the outside of her thighs. As I leaned over her body, I let my bare nipples graze her skin and felt them harden on contact. Gradually, I moved on to the inside of her thighs and that perfect ass as her moans got a little deeper. I was sure she was thoroughly enjoying herself so I let my fingers slide inside her. It was hot and wet just as I was hoping. Her moans were getting louder now. I could tell she was very into it as I slid my fingers in and out of that perfect little hole. Leaning over and whispering in her ear, I asked her if she wanted to turn over.

By this time Jason had moved over to the couch to let us get acquainted. He was stroking that hard cock of his. After all, isn't this the moment men dream about?

As she turned over, I got my first look at her face. She had smooth olive skin, high cheekbones, and the most piercing green eyes with a look of innocence hidden in there somewhere. As we made eye contact she kind of half-smiled in a dreamy sort of way. If she was shy—as Jason had claimed, she certainly wasn't showing it at all.

I leaned down over her to kiss her. The feel of a woman is unmistakable. It's so soft and serene. Our breasts were touching; our hips rocking in unison. I kissed my way down to her neck, supporting her head with one hand and taking her breast in the other. I teasingly flicked my tongue over her nipple before taking it into my mouth. She arched her back and let out another soft moan. Oh yes, she was into it. I slid down further but slowly as to tease her, making her wait, making her want. It was as if she had been waiting her entire lifetime for this very moment, to feel the touch of another woman, to have a woman feel her. I cupped her breast in my hand while the fingers of my other hand grazed her clitoris and then slid inside her again—first one finger and then the other.

In the background I could hear Jason reaching his breaking point. I heard his guttural groan and "Oh shit!" as he came. I felt some satisfaction from that.

I finally gave into her want, to her desire. I let my tongue dance around her clitoris. I had to hold her hips down with one hand to keep her from squirming away with pleasure. As my fingers played with her nice, tight, wet pussy she let out a long moan and I was in heaven. I felt Jason's hands on my hips as he thrust that hard cock into me from behind. I almost fell over. I loved the taste of her in my mouth and the feel of him inside me. As he was fucking me, I was bringing her to that point of no return. She started bucking back and forth on my fingers. I had to keep moving my mouth to keep it on her clit. She was getting wetter with each thrust. As she started to reach her point of ecstasy I moved faster and harder. She was cumming now, her body shivering from the excitement. As she lay there, I reached behind me to get Jason to stop. I wanted to see him fuck her. I wanted to watch, to take it all in.

I gave her another kiss as she was still catching her breath so she could taste herself on my tongue. Then I moved over to Jason's spot on the couch as he entered her. As she wrapped her legs around him and took him in I touched myself. God, I was wet. As he fucked her, harder and harder, she never took her eyes off me. I brought myself to climax just as he was filling her with his second orgasm of the night.

We were all silent for a time, too burnt out to speak or move. He spoke first with the only words he could mutter.

"That was awesome," he said.

She and I both giggled like little schoolgirls. As we started to get dressed, they both thanked me for the wonderful night. "No, no," I said, "Thank you!"

I said my goodbyes and left. I wanted to give them some time to be alone, to talk about the experience they had just had, and as I drove home that night, I realized I had never even gotten her name.

Laurie has been an Athena's Goddess since May of 2009. She received the recognition of Athena's Top New Goddess of 2009. She loves her life, and loves her job. With Athena's as part of her life the possibilities are endless.

Breaking My Own Rules

By Adonis Angel Maldonado Lopez

When we met a few weeks earlier, I had never thought he would be the kind of person that I would be interested in. But that evening we had been talking about many things. I heard about his party life—those days when he went to the nightclubs constantly, acting like he owned them, and how everyone wanted to touch his sculptured ivory, toned body. The more he told me about his life, the more curious I became. I have to admit that it excited me to think about the adventures that we could have together.

On that hot summer night, I could not help but feel aroused when his voice on the phone kept introducing ideas in my head that I secretly wanted to fulfill. Without telling him, I decided to undress and start touching myself. I slowly explored my perspiring olive skin starting with my chest, progressively caressing my stomach, and eventually reaching my engorged member, which was definitely clamoring for attention.

He must have heard my breathing getting heavy. All of a sudden, the topic of our conversation morphed into a more erotic one as we started talking about our desires. I was very shy and reserved, but like any other man, my fantasies could get really detailed in my head.

We both decided to get each other more and more aroused by telling each other what to do, what to touch and when.

He was very dominant in the conversation, and I, being used to constantly controlling everything, felt like this would be one of those times when it would be a good idea to let go and follow. As his sensual voice kept instructing me to stroke my member, telling me to go up, and down, and up, and down with my hand following the rhythm of his words, I felt a rush that I had never felt before. I wanted to be there. My loins were craving attention and at that point I would have given anything to get relief.

As I was playing with my manhood and listening to his voice teasing my curiosity over the phone, he made a suggestion that, at three in the morning, seemed quite farfetched. It went against my self-controlling and prudent nature; it broke all my rules. I quietly listened as he told me that he wished that I could somehow drive all the way down to his house, 45 minutes away, and then we would drive to a secluded place where he would let me for the first time in our still new affair, be the one who penetrated *him*. I laughed nervously, and then when he insisted that he was serious, I thought about how to make it happen.

I was highly aroused by the idea of invading his always reserved and protected anus with my dick. In the few weeks that we had been going out, he always spoke about how he never enjoyed it and how many other men had tried to but he would not allow it. Once we started having sex, as I started falling for him, I felt that I wanted to change many things about his attitude. I wanted to change his "I'm the man who fucks others" attitude. This was my new priority. For the first time in a long time, my mind was flooded by the quickly expanding cloud of lust that overtook me and led me to what happened next.

I had to make this happen. I thought about a way to get there. Having recently moved to the area living on a student's stipend, I did not have a car—but my roommate at the time did. However, he never allowed me to drive it, so I would have to figure out a way to sneak away with it.

Caught up in our conversation about the fantasy that we were building together, I said, "What if I use my roommate's car and drive there right now?"

He immediately responded that that would be really hot and he would make it worth the trip.

I hesitated. I had class the next day at nine in the morning. Driving 45 minutes to pick him up in a practically stolen car, and then driving another half hour to get to the woods, do the deed, drop him off and then get home to shower and make it to class on time seemed like too complex a way to start the day. Over all, it was against anything that I would normally do for anyone. But then I thought: "What the hell— I'm going to do this for myself!"

At 3:30 in the morning, with a raging hard on, and with my desire for his ass all stirred up, I stole my roommate's car and drove to my lover's house. Dressed in light clothes, he jumped in the car and gave me a jug of some sort of alcoholic concoction he said would take the edge off. I could tell he had already had a few drinks before I picked him up, probably to prepare himself for what was coming. He told me to get on the highway and head south where we could go into a park he knew would be private, and we could complete our escapade.

The woods were over a half hour away and he was worried that the excitement could wear down while we drove. So he asked me to open my pants. I had never done anything like this, especially while driving, but I thought: "Oh well, I've come this far."

He lowered his head onto my crotch, and suddenly I felt his luscious lips wrapped around the head of my penis. As they slid down the shaft, his tongue teased my glans and foreskin. While he hungrily moved my member in, and out, and in, and out again of his wet mouth. I grinned and moaned in pleasure while trying to get us to our destination alive.

We finally arrived at the woods and parked in a secluded clearing between the trees. He asked me to get out of the car and directed me to a spot by the lake where the act was going to take place. He threw down a blanket and out of a small bag, he took out some lubricant and a pair of handcuffs. I was not so sure about how those were going to be used, and I was very eager to find out.

We started kissing and as I tasted his succulent lips and rolled my tongue around his mouth teasing him as he teased me, his right hand slipped under my shirt caressing my lower back. He pulled me against him and I could feel his hard, throbbing member press against mine.

We took off our shirts and I could feel his skin moist and sweaty on this hot summer night. I undid the tie in his shorts as I could not wait to feel his erect penis in my hands. First I cupped his testicles, which were warm and hung low. After playing with them for a bit, I caressed his shaft and suddenly I felt a drop of delicious precum leaking out of the head of his member. I knew I was going to get to infiltrate his most private part soon, but I really wanted to enjoy this moment.

I let his pants drop as we stood there, and with my ravenous mouth I tasted his salty neck, nibbled on his small pink but erect nipples and drifted across his belly until I found the treat of his manhood. With the tip of my tongue I tasted the precum that was now slowly flowing out of his penis, and inch by inch, took it all in my mouth. As his delicious shaft went in, and out, and in, and out of my mouth, I could hear his breathing become heavy, leading into a quiet moaning. He was getting close to ecstasy and I knew this was my chance.

I picked up the handcuffs he brought, and asked him to lie on his back by a thin tree. I straddled him and to keep him entertained while I thought of what I was going to do, I lowered my testicles onto his mouth, where he immediately took them in. Cradling both of them in his warm, moist mouth and caressing them with his lips distracted me briefly, but then my purpose came back to me. I wanted to dominate him, show him that it doesn't take "being a man" to make a man. I wrapped his arms around the trunk of the tree and quickly secured them. There he lay, on his back, legs spread, dominated, helpless, with his alabaster skin naked and me with all the power.

I still wanted him to enjoy being penetrated, so first I started caressing his pink, tight anus with a finger. As I looked at it, I couldn't help but wonder what it would taste like. I knew from our past encounters that he always cleaned up before, so without hesitation, I lowered my mouth onto it and started rimming it. The fleshy taste, seasoned only by his salty sweat, was quite arousing and made me extremely impatient to finally invade him with my penis.

Excited that I was going to finally have my chance, I grabbed the bottle of Wet Silicone® lubricant, put some on my right hand and massaged my member with it. Then I leisurely teased his anus with my penis, and as the head rubbed against it, I felt his eagerness to be defiled. Unhurriedly, while I held his legs up with one hand, with the other I guided my shaft into his now greedy opening, the sphincter relaxed and welcomed my incursion. I lowered his legs so they would wrap around my waist, and I was now close enough to kiss him. With each thrust in and out, and in, and out of him, I felt us become closer, and now more than a conquest, it was a life-changing experience that would define our relationship.

As he groaned, I kept going—in, and out, and in, and out again— leading to an ecstasy I had never felt before. While all that was happening, I also managed to play with his penis. Stroking it up, and down, and up, and down, getting him close to climax. The intense expression on his face was priceless and suddenly with a loud scream that probably traveled over the water to the other side of the lake, his cum jetted over his shoulder and hit the tree that helped restrain him. At the same time, I got to release my seed inside of him, filling his cavity with me, leaving the ultimate evidence of my triumph. We were now even. We were now one.

I released him from his cuffs, and we laid for a bit on a pile of leaves by the water. The sun started gracing us with its light, signaling that a new day was starting. And indeed it was a new day, a new life where I had for the first time in a long time broken my own rules.

We headed back so I could make it to my class, but all I could think about was this mad moment of lust. What started as a simple erotic phone conversation taught me to let go. And by letting go, I found love.

Angel has been an Adonis since 2009 and has fun doing parties for his very diverse customers. He strives to help them open their minds and enjoy their intimacy to the maximum. He's a devoted partner and passionate about life.

Element of Surprise

By Goddess Sherry Harmon

"Do you trust me?" I asked looking up at Pete from between his legs. My hand stilled on his cock as I waited for an answer.

He laughed nervously. "Why?"

"Just answer! Do you?"

"Of course."

I smiled up at him and resumed my slow stroke up and down his shaft.

"Mmm," he half moaned and half sighed as he leaned back against the pillows on the bed. "I love when you tease me."

"I know," I said. With the other hand I pulled out the four-inch anal vibrator I had hidden earlier.

Putting the vibrator down on the bed next to me, I groped for the bottle of WET® lubricant I had also hidden earlier. Pete was completely oblivious; his eyes were closed, and I could see he was totally absorbed in the feeling of my hand teasing his cock.

It was difficult to lube the vibrator with only one hand, but I was determined. I didn't want to lose the element of surprise, so I made sure my hand never faltered its slide along his skin.

When I had the vibe ready, I leaned over his cock and wrapped my mouth around it. Very slowly, I eased down his shaft, swallowing him inch by inch. He groaned. I had just learned to deep throat, and he was still surprised each time that I was able to hold all of his cock in my mouth. I was also surprised every time by the thrill it gave me to be able to swallow him.

I caressed his balls with my free hand and slid my mouth back up to the tip of his cock. I teased the head with my tongue, listening to Pete's sharp breaths. I loved to tease and torment him, alternating soft licks with deep throating, fast strokes with slow slides of the tongue.

On the next downward slide of my mouth, I teased the tip of the vibrator around his anus. I knew he would think it was my finger since I had done that before. Gently I began to push the lubed vibrator into his ass. I felt him tighten around it and his legs tensed at the intrusion.

I began a more vigorous rhythm of my mouth on his dick to distract him from his tension. Slowly, I eased the vibe in as far as I could.

I looked up at Pete's face when I turned the vibrator on. His eyes flew open in surprise, and again his muscles tensed.

"Wha…?" he began to question, but the words died as I increased the speed of the vibrator and began a steady in and out rhythm.

"I am going to fuck you in the ass with this vibrator," I told him, kissing and licking his balls between each word. "And I'm going to suck your cock while I do it."

"Oh God," he moaned.

In and out, I slid the vibrator. I could feel myself getting wetter. I was so aroused by the power I had, knowing I was fucking his ass, knowing he was completely vulnerable to me. I wrapped my mouth around his cock, tighter than before, and matched the pace of my mouth to the vibe. In and out, up and down, over and over.

My clitoris throbbed; I needed to be touched so badly, but more than that, I wanted Pete to come. It didn't take long for me to get my wish. Pete's hips began to lift from the bed as he tried to fuck my mouth. I let him; my mouth accepted his thrusts as I continued the plunge of the vibrator with my hand.

"Oh God," he yelled, his hands holding tight to my hair. His cock was so far into my mouth that when he came I didn't even taste it.

I switched off the vibrator and slid it out of Pete's ass. He released my hair and I lifted my head and grinned up at him.

"You're a naughty girl," he told me. I could tell he was still trying to catch his breath, and I was pleased that I had given him such pleasure.

My grin widened. "I know."

"You know what happens to naughty girls, don't you?"

I looked down at the bed, trying to appear remorseful, but I wasn't. I knew what he meant, and though it seemed impossible that he could arouse me anymore than I had been while fucking and sucking him, his question alone nearly made me cum in anticipation. Several minutes passed as he continued to watch me. I grew eager to know what he would do to me, and I knew that he waited not only so he could recover from his orgasm, but more so that he could torture me with his silence.

"On your hands and knees." His voice was quiet, but commanding.

I quickly complied; my body tingled as I waited for what I knew was coming. And then, when I had begun to relax—smack! A sharp crack on my ass as he spanked me. Smack! Smack! His hand fell hard on each cheek and the burn of it sent shivers through me. I loved to be spanked, to feel that quick burst of pain as flesh met flesh. Again and again, his hand struck me until I knew my ass was red from the blows.

Behind me, I heard movement, but I didn't dare turn to look. Besides, the anticipation, the waiting, only increased my arousal. And then, I felt him behind me, one of his hands tight on my hips while the other spread my legs further apart. Without warning, I felt his cock pushing into my anus. I was so surprised, I cried out. Always before he had taken his time with anal sex and made sure that I was relaxed and ready for him.

Pete reached his hand underneath me and began to tease my clit. Automatically I began to relax around his cock as I focused on the pleasure in my clit. Taking advantage, he slid completely into me. Now that I had adjusted to him being inside me, I could tell that he had at least taken the time to use lube before he had so suddenly entered me. I knew I should have been upset with him, but I wasn't. I was just as turned on being under his control as I had been having control over him.

Pete played his fingers along my clit as he thrust in and out of me. Finally he whispered in my ear, "Cum."

He held his fingers tight against my clit, the way I liked it and plunged deep into me.

"Cum for me," he said again, and then he moaned as his own orgasm took him.

Hearing his command, feeling his hand on my clit, and even more, feeling his cock pulsing in my ass, I shattered in climax, my whole body trembling from the pleasure of it. Pete was barely able to pull his cock out of me before we both collapsed onto the bed. He lay draped over me, his hand idly playing with my hair.

I turned to face him. "So…does that mean you liked it?" I asked, with a sleepy smile.

He laughed. "What do you think?"

Sherry is a Goddess who started her Athena's Home Novelties business in 2010. She believes that all acts of love and pleasure are sacred. She is a loving wife and a good-humored woman who loves to educate adults regarding sexual health.

The Orthopedist's Wife

By Goddess Angela Goldsberry

I am the bored wife of a prominent orthopedic surgeon. I am rich, beautiful, and lonely. I have too much time on my hands and too few interests to fill it. I am a slave to my husband's career: expected to appear and play the dutiful hostess when called, relegated to the background when convenient.

My husband isn't home enough to be good to me. Surgeries, rounds, conventions, racquetball, drinks and whores keep him occupied. I'm not supposed to know, but I do. I'm supposed to care, but I don't. As long as he keeps me in the style to which I've become accustomed, he's free to do as he pleases.

We keep up appearances. It's an unspoken bargain between us. Sex ended long ago, but neither of us minds. He has his own "interests" and I'm happy to be free of his soft, pasty hands probing me—examining me—like one of his cadaveric specimens he uses when teaching.

Spending his money is my favorite pastime, especially when it leads to other—shall we say—sports. Currently, I'm having the attic turned into a loft. No special reason. It's just one more opportunity to waste the earnings of the MDiety. And I'm wasting them well.

The two men who have been here for the past few weeks are certainly a treat for the senses. Frank is a compact, tawny-maned electrician, slight of build, but muscular. His jeans are tight and well worn, the bulge behind his zipper foretells a fulfilling experience. I speculate as to whether his face sees a razor much. More importantly, I wonder what that stubble would feel like on my thighs.

Then there's Vince—a giant with a curtain of black hair that falls halfway down his back. His aquamarine eyes are plasma-hot and mesmerizing. As a carpenter, he is frequently lifting heavy loads, the muscles of his chest constantly rippling and expanding. I get wet just watching him move.

I spent days deliberating over which of them I wanted and planning a private rendezvous. Then, genius struck me: why not have them both?

So, here I sit, idle in my kitchen while they toil away overhead. I'm wearing my tightest, shortest cutoffs, a button-down top, and a bra— no panties. I wriggle in my chair, hypersensitive to all the stimuli—the seam of my cutoffs massaging my clit, the lace of my bra scratching my nipples. I can hardly stand the wait. I've given the men free run of the house, and they've developed a reliable routine, including lunch in the kitchen at noon. It's now 11:47.

I'm getting really fidgety when I hear footsteps—one set, not two. It's Frank. This is different. I wonder where Vince is and how long it will be before he joins us. I busy myself at the sink, doing dishes while Frank slyly checks out my ass. I stretch, thrusting my rear out as if to ask, "Do you like?" He clears his throat self-consciously and I know he does.

He sits at the table and starts to unpack his lunch. He may be ready to eat, but food is the last thing he wants. I coyly peek over my shoulder, and he boldly returns my stare. He knows exactly what I'm up to.

"Do you have any ketchup?" he asks conversationally. Oh, this is rich.

"I'm not sure," I reply, playing along. "I'll check."

I fetch a stepladder from the pantry and set it up directly opposite Frank. I search the cupboard thoroughly for his unimportant, nonexistent ketchup, twisting, turning, bending, reaching. Then I feel a warm hand on the back of my thigh.

"Need some help?"

I move down a step. Frank's hand slides up my leg, stopping briefly at my ass before sliding forward. My pussy is swollen and refuses to be contained by the tiny wet crotch of my shorts. Frank leisurely caresses the exposed flesh with seductive fingers. I turn to face him, leaning back and spreading my legs slightly so he can see my cunt runneth over.

"I don't seem to have any ketchup," I tell him with a devilish smile, "but could I interest you in some hot sauce?"

Frank laughs and the rich timbre of his voice makes me quiver. He palms my mound again and I gently close my legs on his fingers, trapping them against my pussy. Using his pinioned hand as a lever, he pulls me forward. I fall against him willingly, filling his face with my tits. A growl rumbles in his throat and he dips his head, tonguing my cleavage as he lifts me into his arms and deposits me on the table behind us.

Stubble rasps against my neck and cheek as Frank trails a path of fire to my mouth. The bristles are soft, not stiff. His stiffness is all in his jeans, I observe wryly, parting my lips to greedily inhale his probing tongue.

His hands are exquisitely rough on my flesh as he fumbles with my blouse. Frustrated, he rips the blouse and bra down the center. Buttons hit the floor unnoticed as his warm hands capture my tits, kneading the globes, tracing circles around the areolae with his thumbs and tugging the nipples with his fingertips.

His mouth releases mine in want of my breasts and he worships them with his lips, tongue, and teeth. I'm already in heaven, and I want more. When his fingers pop the snap on my shorts and slide the zipper down, there's no going back.

"Eat me," I whisper hotly. "Eat my pussy!"

I rest my elbows on the table and lift my hips so that Frank can remove my shorts. He throws off his shirt and steps between my legs, pressing his bulge against my naked pussy. He returns his mouth to my body, kissing, licking, and sucking his way from my neck to my crotch. I hear his hum of approval as he beholds my glistening sex. Almost reverently, he places a gentle kiss on the closed folds. Then he begins to tongue me, nudging my petals open so that he can taste my honey.

"Do you like that?" he murmurs, working a finger, then two into my tight, steaming hole.

"Yes," I whimper, as he slides his fingers slowly in and out. "God, yes!"

He spreads my lips with his thumb, caressing his way to my clit, and then replaces his fingers with his mouth. As soon as I feel his tongue inside me, I cum—hard. He affixes his lips to my clit, sucking on the pulsing button and almost immediately, I climax again.

"I was going to ask you if you started eating without me," says a voice from behind us. "But the answer is obvious."

I wonder if Vince finds us comical—me spread-eagled on the table with Frank seated before me, feasting on my pussy. But when he wordlessly shifts his stiffening cock into a more comfortable position, I know he finds this anything but funny.

"Is this a private game or can anyone play?"

I wink at him invitingly and he quickly loses his shirt. He works the zipper of his pants and, as he comes around the other side of the table to stand before me, he pulls his big cock free.

"Here you go," Vince offers politely and I accept happily.

I suck and lick him until he is granite. He holds my head, his hands tangled in my hair as he fucks my mouth. Then he has me roll onto my stomach, legs dangling over the edge of table, so that I can suck him more easily.

Frank has been watching us, and I now see that his cock is out too. My ass contracts excitedly as I watch him stroke himself. I turn back to Vince and proceed to go down on him in earnest. At first, I devour his cockhead like a lollipop, swirling my tongue all around the smooth knob. Then I do the shaft, licking it and sliding my lips over it, slowly, leisurely, tauntingly. Finally, much to Vince's surprise, I practically swallow him whole.

"That's it." he groans, pushing deeply into my mouth. "Suck it. Oh yeah! Suck it!"

A whimper catches in my throat when Frank lightly brushes my pussy with the head of his cock. He teases me, moving just out of reach if I try for more solid contact. I hope he doesn't make me beg. On second thought, I hope he does. Finally, he presses against my syrupy fuckhole and works his way in, one glorious push at a time.

Upon full penetration, he sighs with satisfaction and stands still, savoring my tightness, allowing me to enjoy the fullness. Then he moves, gyrating in a slow, primitive groove. He massages my ass roughly and when he presses his thumb against my rosy pucker, I don't protest. I take him in, grinding against his hand. His balls start slapping my pussy as he fucks me harder. I'm moaning and it's getting hard to keep Vince's cock in my mouth. I'm ready to cum again, but first, I have an idea.

Extricating myself from my fuckmates, I take Vince by the hand and sit him on the stepladder, straddling it like a horse. In turn, I mount Vince and span his thighs, the rungs of the ladder like stirrups. I position myself over his sizable erection and then slowly impale myself. I ride Vince like a mechanical bull, pistoning on his hot cock while he palms my ass in his huge hands. He spreads my cheeks, exposing my anal wink to Frank who doesn't miss his cue. Frank slides three fingers into my mouth, forcing me to suck them until they're soaked. He then uses them to prep my ass, fingering me with one until my tight opening is relaxed, then adding the second and third.

"Fuck me." I beg him as I continue to bounce on Vince's cock. "Please fuck my ass!"

He doesn't need to be told twice. Slowly, he pushes his cock into my ass, working me, stretching me, and then inching in up to his balls.

I can't believe this! Here I am, in my kitchen with two total strangers, a cock in my cunt, and one in my ass. I never imagined that this was possible! I feel so deliciously full! As we fuck, Vince continues to knead my ass and Frank does likewise with my tits.

"Harder!" I cry. I'll be sporting bruises in the morning, but I don't care. I slide a hand down my body so that I can rub my clit and the men are all encouragement.

"Do it, baby," Vince whispers.

"That's it," Frank agrees, tonguing my ear. "Play with that pussy!"

And I do. My pussy convulses in orgasm, squeezing the two cocks inside me, coaxing them to join me. Frank goes next, spewing hot semen in my ass with a roar.

"I want to cum in your mouth." Vince breathes against my lips. I nod my consent. He eases me off Frank and then lifts me off his own cock. I get down on my knees and take him in hand.

"Lick it," he commands. I obey. "Now, suck your juice off my cock."

I groan and take him between my lips. The tang of my own pussy makes me want to cum again. I start to finger my dripping pussy and Frank is right there, taking over so that I can concentrate on sucking Vince.

"Oh, yes," Vince purrs. "Make me cum!"

It doesn't take long. A few good slurps and his load spills down my throat, his cock pulsating for what seems like an eternity. At last, he drops to the floor and watches Frank stroke me to one more thundering orgasm.

Totally spent, I sink to the floor, sucking my nectar from Frank's fingers. Miraculously, he starts to grow hard again. Not to be outdone, Vince begins manhandling his cock too. At this rate, the attic may never get finished!

Angela has been a Goddess since 2009, and a secret writer of erotica for many more. She enjoys dispelling sexual taboos by presenting sex as healthy and exciting. Sexy husband, Tom, and two wonderful children make her life complete.

Part Two

Mystery

Sex without ties—the figurative ones—is the perfect fallback fantasy. Are you up for an anonymous romp? Of course you are! Contrary to the song, sometimes you want to go where no one knows your name.

Mystery Girl By By Goddess Molly Whitman   43

Pancakes By Goddess Carmen dePina   47

Lavender Diamond By Goddess Barbara Rutenkroger   53

The Stranger By Goddess Alicia Orlow   59

Mystery Girl

By Goddess Molly Whitman

Last night, When my friends invited me to the club, I thought I'd just have a few beers and dance a bit. I was still feeling depressed about my recent breakup. I didn't think I'd wake up with another woman beside me in bed, but here she is.

I don't want to disturb her sleep, especially not until I figure out who she is and what happened last night. I look around the room for clues—two wines glasses on the night stand; one—no two—empty bottles of red wine; stylish black heels my clumsy feet could never pull off; a leopard-print bra—not mine—draped over a chair. It looks like we had a good time. In my half-awake daze, I remember that she is still beside me and turn to search her body for more clues.

Her blond, curly locks spread across the pillow, and being careful not to wake her, I gently brush her hair back to reveal her beautiful face. She has white, creamy skin and a flawless complexion. Although she is asleep, her pursed red lips give the impression that she is waiting for a kiss. My eyes travel downward. I am scared that she may wake to find me staring. My heartbeat quickens as I begin to tingle with arousal. She has perfect, absolutely perfect tits. The nipples are hard and pink, creating a stark contrast against her milky flesh. Her breasts look like heavenly pillows. I want to nuzzle in them and feel their weight in my hands. Dare I look further?

I cannot stop myself. She has a petite, athletic physique and a flower tattoo on her hip, which playfully leads my gaze to the triangular mound between her legs. She is wearing white panties, and my mouth begins to water as I think of what must lay underneath. Suddenly, she rolls toward me, so I shut my eyes for fear of being found out. Who knows what she will think of me, now that our inhibitions are no longer suppressed by alcohol?

"Hello, gorgeous," she purrs. Well, at least she seems to like me.

"You were quite the aggressive one last night, weren't you?" she teases.

I don't really remember, but the sight of her body so relaxed, so comfortable in my bed, assures me I did a great job. I open my eyes to meet hers. She moves closer to me, her fabulous breasts brushing lightly against mine through my T-shirt. My nipples harden as well, revealing my excitement.

To my surprise, she reaches between my legs to feel my wetness. A shiver runs up and down my spine, and I grow wetter from the touch of her fingers on the awakened nerves in my skin. My pulse quickens, and I swallow hard. She teases me for a moment, tracing her fingers around the lips of my vagina before finally plunging them deep inside me. I'm on my back now, so it is easy to stretch my legs over her shoulders.

I let myself enjoy the moment, no longer concerned with figuring out the mystery of who she is and what happened last night. She kisses my stomach, just below my navel, torturing me with hints of pleasure. Her lips feel so good I could let her do this all day. But she knows what I want and soon shifts her focus to my aching pussy.

She senses I want her to eat me, so she buries her head between my legs. I gather her yellow curls in my hand so my view of her licking my pussy is no longer obstructed. With her hair still clenched in my hand, I begin to pump my hips up and down with the rhythm of her tongue, which she darts in and out of her mouth as if she were licking an ice cream cone. She places three fingers inside me and licks her lips before starting on my clitoris again. Her gentle tongue feels slippery and wet and provides a delicious contrast to the power of her fingers.

I begin to moan, growing close to orgasm. I feel my muscles tighten around her fingers, squeezing and pulsing with her every movement. Just when I feel like I'm about to cum, she lifts her head and spins around so that her toned ass is right in my face. She positions herself over my mouth and lowers onto me so I may taste the sweet juice already wetting her swollen pink lips. I take her into my mouth, thrusting my tongue inside of her as deep as it can go. This is only my second encounter with a woman (except what I don't remember from last night), and I worry that I won't get her to cum as quickly as she will do for me. However, she soon begins to moan and shake from my pulsating tongue.

The deep, guttural sounds she makes turn me on even more. I press my tongue hard against her clit, massaging it faster and faster. Just as my legs begin to shake and I am on the verge of coming, she cries out, "Make me cum baby!"

I can only manage a grunt of my own and instead focus on plunging my tongue inside her to taste as much as I can. I hold my breath slightly as I orgasm, heightening the sensation and prolonging this moment that I never want to end. She climaxes at the same time, as we both continue to lick and finger furiously, giving in completely to our bliss.

She collapses on top of me for a second, leaving me to stare once more at her flawless ass. She sits up and moves to lie on my chest, supported by my arm under her head. She looks so serene; we lie there for several minutes, and I try not to move my arm for fear that she will turn away. I love the feeling of her skin pressed against mine.

I do not say a word, not wishing to reveal the fact that I do not remember her name. I want to tell her that this is not just a one-night stand. I feel something more. But I must get the courage to ask. I look down and she meets my gaze with a warm, comfortable smile. I rehearse the words in my head one last time. I close my eyes for a final moment of serenity. As I open them and prepare my speech, she asks, "So, what's your name, anyway?"

Molly Whitman joined Athena's in 2009. She is a Goddess whose bubbly personality and passion for her business make her parties must-attend events. She attends law school in Dallas, Texas and lives with her fiancée, Sarah, and her mini daschund, Darcy.

Pancakes

By Goddess Carmen dePina

For many people, lazy Sunday mornings mean kitchens filled with the scent of freshly cooked pancakes, laced with butter and maple syrup. Not me. Lazy Sunday mornings remind me of a tall, dark man with smooth dark chocolate-colored skin topped off with a smile as sweet as whipped cream. He was delicious to look at and sweeter to taste.

It was the beginning of summer. The air was still crisp but not cool. I started my day walking my dog. I walked the same route, the same time, everyday. I'd walk past a house where I noticed a man sitting on his porch. He seemed to be enjoying the quiet sounds of the city in that time before everyone else wakes up. It's very peaceful. I looked at him and he smiled. His lips parted to reveal a perfect, pearly white smile. I had to stop myself from gazing too long. I looked away and as I continued walking, I felt his eyes watching me, moving over my hips. I glanced behind me to still see that smile. I smiled back, thinking to myself, I know what that smile means.

The next day I continued my daily routine. It was warmer than the day before but I didn't mind. I followed my route and the man on the porch was standing at the edge of his driveway. He was taller than

I figured he'd be, a foot taller than I am to be exact. He smiled and waved as I walked toward him. He was wearing a tank top and jeans. I can tell he spent a lot of time in the gym because his arms looked like they belong to an NFL player. I was a little nervous as I approached him and I started to feel as warm as the sun that glistened on his dark skin.

"Good morning," he said.

His voice was softer than I imagined but very soothing. There goes that smile again.

"Good morning," I reply.

I look up at him and meet his eyes. I feel as though he can see through me. I feel naked with this man looking at me and strangely I'm okay with that. I have no defenses. My stomach feels empty and nervous, but I can't look away from him. I put my hands in my pocket to keep them from sweating.

"I see you every morning, and I can't help but notice you. My name is Aaron."

I continue to look at him. Despite being mesmerized by the definition of his chest through his shirt, I regain my composure and introduce myself.

"My name is Carmen. So do you always introduce yourself to random women walking their dogs?"

He laughed. "No, only to women who have a smile like yours."

I can feel myself blushing. I look away and say thank you.

As I walk away, he says "So I'll see you tomorrow? Same time, same place?"

I nod.

The next day, he met me at the end of his driveway again. This time, he asked to walk with me. I obliged. How could I not. This man was beautiful. We talked and laughed. It seemed very comfortable. We continued this routine for a month and while we became familiar to one another, there was no denying that there was an attraction that was obvious when we were around each other. We had a connection.

Every morning at the end of our walk it was more painful to leave him. I wanted to know what his lips felt like against mine. I wanted to experience his strong arms wrap around my waist and pull me toward him. As comfortable as we were, we never mentioned how much we wanted each other. It was an unspoken truth but I wasn't sure how much longer it could remain that way.

One rainy morning, I left for my walk not expecting to see Aaron. I felt a little sad because I looked forward to seeing him. As I hurried along, I saw him standing in the rain right where we met every morning. The rain soaked his shirt making the outline of his incredibly sculpted chest more visible. He waited for me to approach him. I couldn't look away. I knew something was different about how he was looking at me.

I finally reached him and without saying a word, he looked deeply into my eyes, took the dog's leash in one hand, my hand in the other and led me into the house. Once we entered the doorway and shut the door behind us, he dropped the dog's leash, cupped my face with his hands and began kissing me.

I felt his kiss in every girlish region of my body. This moment had built up over a month. I licked my lips, savoring the taste his lips left behind. I could feel my nipples become erect and blood rushing throughout my body. As our wet bodies pressed against one another, I could feel his erection grow. I wondered if I would be able to accommodate someone of his size. I'm sure I could make it work somehow.

He began stripping off my wet clothes, and I feverishly tore at his. He scooped me up in his arms and carried me over to his sofa. As he laid me down, we never broke our gaze. I had never felt so connected to someone before. He proceeded to kiss me again, moving down my chin and neck. His hands reached for mine and he guided them to feel his excitement. I really began to worry because it seemed much bigger than my original observation. But my vagina was saying, "Don't worry. We can handle this."

He continued tracing my body with his lips, sucking my nipples, gently biting them and licking them with his tongue. My body agreed. My vagina was throbbing, begging to be penetrated. He moved further down and grabbed my legs and put them over his shoulders. He lowered his head until his mouth came in contact with my clitoris. I felt an explosion of pleasure as he tasted my sweetness. His tongue flicked furiously. My body felt as though it was going to buckle from the amount of pleasure he was providing. He looked up at me and licked his lips as to savor his treat.

I sat up and returned the favor by removing his boxer shorts to expose his fully engorged penis. I began sucking the tip of his penis slowly. I ran my tongue around it before easing more of the penis into my mouth. I ran my tongue down his penis, stroking it with my hand. I could feel him throbbing in my mouth. As I stroked him up and down, the rain seemed to beat harder against the window as though demanding more.

I felt him wanting to explode, but he didn't. Instead he stopped me and laid me down again. He laid down on top of me and without any manual assistance he entered my vagina. I felt connected. I didn't want to be anywhere else. Each thrust of his hips led me closer to ecstasy. Our bodies moved with a rhythm that matched my racing heart. I pulled him closer and he penetrated me deeper. He kissed me as though to consume me. I willingly let him try.

He thrust harder and faster, my body felt mini-explosions going off everywhere. I was at sensory overload. My muscles tightened, if I exhaled I would explode all over the room. Our eyes met and we came. Everything released. My ears were ringing. Pure contentment washed over me.

Our bodies were wet, not from rain, but from the passion we just experienced. I lay there with him silently for a few minutes trying to recapture my thoughts. He looked down at me with that smile and asked if I was in the mood for pancakes. I smiled and nodded.

"Pancakes sound great."

Carmen joined Athena's in 2009. She enjoys educating singles and couples about the benefits of sensual exploration. While her journey with Athena's is still just beginning, she is proud to have been able to enhance the lives of the people she has encountered with a very special gift. Carmen is currently single, looking to meet someone who enjoys an occasional breakfast in bed.

The Lavender Diamond

By Goddess Barbara Rutenkroger

Laughter and screams fill the air along with the smells of cotton candy and caramel apples. I'm standing in the midway of the state fair, watching happy people milling around. Watching people is fun. I find a rock wall to sit on and get comfy. This is my night off and I intend to enjoy it by watching people.

It doesn't take long for me to notice someone else doing the same thing. He's sitting about a dozen spaces away, watching the others. I'm fascinated that someone else is a watcher. He has a nice strong build. His muscles are just bulging under his black T-shirt. He has a tattoo on his upper arm that I can't quite make out. Oh well.

I turn back to my people-watching. After a few minutes I feel his gaze on me. I turn and stare into the most beautiful eyes ever. They are a silvery violet that almost glows. His hair is a dark chocolate brown and his mouth is perfect-looking. When he smiles and nods my way, my insides turn liquid and heat rushes to my center. I smile, nod and unconsciously lick my lips wondering if the rest of him looks and tastes as good as this. I would love to have him. He looks at me like he knows what I'm thinking and gives me a slow smile.

I turn back to my people watching and notice a young couple getting hot and heavy in the shadows of the House of Fun ride. They are really getting into each other. His hand goes slowly up her skirt; she spreads her feet farther apart. They are making this ride a true House of Fun. Her hand fumbles with his jean's buttons. After a few minutes of heavy groping and grinding, they must have noticed that they were too out in the open because they suddenly moved further back in the shadows.

I knew there was a nice patch of grass with shrubs to hide behind hidden from view in back of the House of Fun. I was already feeling warm and fuzzy inside from looking at and thinking about my yummy fellow watcher and the young lovers, so I walked around and hid behind the bushes. By the time I reached the bushes, the couple was partially undressed.

It seemed like hands were everywhere. It didn't take long for their clothes to be off. They seemed to slow down a little, or maybe it was just in slow motion for me. Her hands went up his arms and across his chest, over his shoulders, caressing down his back. He was copying her every move except instead of going down her back, his hands came to rest on her breasts. He slowly began circling her nipples and then pulling, lightly pinching and teasing them to be tight buds. She was cupping his balls and massaging the long thick length of him.

I was feeling their pleasure as heat rushed between my legs. I slipped my hand in my pants feeling how wet, hot and slick I was. My other hand went up my shirt to play with my nipple as this young man was doing to his woman.

I was so wrapped up in the scene in front of me and my own reaction that I didn't hear my fellow watcher come up behind me. He circled his strong arms around me and followed my hands to where they were busy on my body, startling me. When I jumped around, I saw the hint of humor and the white-hot desire in his amazing eyes that were turning a darker violet as the heat between us increased. I smiled, sighed and stepped aside so he too could see the scene before us.

The young woman was now on her knees kissing the head of her man's penis while playing with his balls. While she was doing this, I decided to take some initiative of my own. I slowly started to rub my new friend's fly and found he was as ready as the young man in front of us. I got his pants open and was delighted to find he was as good all over as I had thought he would be. While I was enjoying the feeling of his thick length and heaviness, he was peeling my clothes off and soon I was naked before him.

The young man was now on the ground himself and was enjoying feasting on his woman. My mysterious lover decided to match what we were watching. He fell to his knees as he pushed me back. He started kissing, nipping and nibbling at my ears and worked his way down my neck to my aching breasts. He licked one by one ever so slowly getting them each to a hard bud. My insides were so hot, like molten lava. He started moving his mouth over my stomach while lowering his body down onto mine. Soon he was parting my swollen lips and gently blowing on my center. It was a pleasure that I will not soon forget.

As a passing cool breeze hit me, his mouth came behind it to warm me up. He kissed and sucked on my clit as I bucked up into him. He held me still in his arms and his mouth kept me from moving away. I looked over to the young couple who were now greedily licking and sucking at each other's bodies. They had the right idea. I reached for my lover and found to my delight that somehow he had shed his clothes. He moved his lower body to my mouth while still licking me. He knew exactly what I wanted to do. I licked and sucked on his clean-shaven balls, then slowly went up his long shaft, taking him into my hungry mouth. When I sucked him deep and hard it was his turn to buck. He pushed harder into my mouth and the salty taste was telling me he was ready for more.

The thought pushed me over the edge. At that moment he inserted two fingers inside me while sucking my clit hard. Wave after hot wave came crashing through me. Before I landed back on earth he swung me around to where I was under him and he swiftly surged forward, uniting us as one. He slowed his movements causing the tightening and warmth to spread through my lower muscles once again. He knew how to build the tension just right within me. I looked up into those now deep violet eyes and saw mirrored what I felt—white-hot desire building to a crescendo. I broke eye contact and let my gaze fall down his slick chest and continue down to where our clean-shaven bodies connected.

Seeing our bodies so close and intimate put my desire into overdrive as he ever so slowly pulled out until just the very tip of him was left, then plunged forward. I looked over to our entertainment and was fascinated. The young woman flipped her man onto his back and started her own torture on him. I liked that idea. So straightening my leg out while rolling, I ended up on top where I was the one in control. I could see he liked this, his eyes became darker and his nipples became taut and erect. I reached out and rolled them between my fingers; he gasped and gripped my hips tighter. I leaned down and licked on one nipple, then the other, blowing gently across his chest. He swelled even more inside me. I squeezed his cock with my pussy, then started to rock against him.

We continued like that until I wasn't sure who was in control anymore. I reached behind me and played with his balls. His hands were on my breasts pulling, tugging and pinching. With my other hand I found my own pleasure button. What a sight to see, I thought. Our young couple was doing just that—while we were a bit distracted, they had turned and were watching us.

Here I was riding a mysterious lover massaging his balls while rubbing my clit and his hands all over my breasts, pulling my hardened nipples. All this out in the open; I was wanton and didn't even care. It felt so good, so right.

All of a sudden everything clicked at once. I pushed down one last time and demanded the same from him. He felt my climax and pushed even farther. When I stopped stroking my clit because it was so sensitive, he started rubbing it furiously while pumping and pounding into me. I came hard and he followed behind me. I felt his hot spurts singeing my insides. Finally I collapsed on top of him and slid to the side, trying to calm my breathing. I looked up at those beautiful eyes and smiled. He smiled and nodded to where our young couple was laying as we were, exhausted and completely satisfied. I think, as my eyelids became heavy, that this is what I want every night of my life.

A night sound—an owl or car or something—jarred me out of my little nap. I sat up, looking around finding myself staring at myself in my bedroom mirror. What had happened was a dream, I thought drowsily. I sighed and started to get up when I noticed a note on my pillow.

"Meet me in the shower" was all it said. Just the thought made me tingle as I walked to my shower and my violet-eyed man. As I reached down to grasp the doorknob, I looked at my left hand with the lavender diamond and once again thought of the night I met my husband at the state fair.

Barb became a Goddess in 2007. She enjoys doing parties to educate and enlighten adults about their bodies and how to have a fulfilling sex life. She is a loving wife of 20 years, a mother, grandmother, and innovative lover.

The Stranger

By Goddess Alicia Orlow

Ava checked to make sure the doors and windows were all locked up before heading to her room to try and beckon a restful sleep. She'd had the strange feeling of being watched over the past few days, and her sleep had been fitful at best. As Ava finally settled into bed, she hoped sleep would come quickly tonight. She pulled the blankets over her body and turned out the light. After a short time, she drifted off.

Sometime later, Ava awoke with a start. Again, she had that feeling of being watched. Just as she had done the previous nights, she scanned the room, which was dimly lit by outside lights, but saw nothing unusual. Suddenly, Ava heard a small sound and sensed movement in the corner of the room. She froze. She wanted to run or scream, but she knew it was unlikely she'd be able to get out. She turned toward that corner of the room and could make out a shadowy silhouette. She readied her body to fight off an attack.

The silhouette in the shadows began to move toward her. Ava's heart and breathing raced. The man had a tall, muscular build, which worried her as she tried to figure out how to fight him off. Just as she was about to spring from her bed, he began to talk quietly to her.

"Ava, please do not be afraid," he said in a smooth, velvety, deep voice. "I will never hurt you. On the contrary, I want only to bring you pleasure." His words poured over her body like silk.

Ava thought about running, but found herself paralyzed. Her body wouldn't budge. The stranger walked slowly toward her, and he reached out his hand to touch her body through the covers. The moment his hand made contact with her, Ava was filled with warmth and all fear melted from her body. She trembled slightly but not from fear. The stranger slowly pulled the blankets from the bed and Ava's exposed skin began to tingle.

"Ava, you are so beautiful. I have been wanting to touch you for so long."

"Who are you?" Ava asked, breathlessly.

"It is not important who I am. Just know that I will adore and pleasure every inch of your body if you'll let me." His voice was like satin running over her skin.

Ava thought she should resist but found herself mesmerized by his deep, hypnotic voice and gentle touch. The stranger leaned down at the foot of her bed. He started at her ankles and slowly, gently licked and kissed his way up the inside of her legs. As he moved up her body, he slowly pushed her legs open wider to more fully expose the center of her pleasure. Her pussy began to get wet and ache.

The stranger skimmed his soft lips over her panties and then made his way up over her stomach and to her breasts. Ava couldn't contain the moan that escaped from her mouth as he continued to tease her body with his magnificent lips and tongue. Her stranger slowly sucked one nipple into his wet mouth while he ran his fingers up her thigh and stomach. Then he gently touched her pussy through her panties, which was now dripping in anticipation of his iron-hard cock that she could feel rubbing lightly against her thigh. Ava needed this man inside her.

He slowly moved down and removed her panties. He opened her up with his fingers and made one long, luxurious lick from her opening to her clit. Then he gently sucked her clit into his mouth where he brought her to the brink of climax—then released it. He did it again, but this time he put two, then three fingers inside her pussy and, again, brought her to the edge of ecstasy.

Finally, when she thought she couldn't take any more, he brought her over the edge. Her body shook as it exploded in ecstasy. As she began to recover, he covered her body with his and drove his thick, iron-hard cock into her dripping, wet pussy. He kissed her deeply while he drove himself over and over into her, bringing them closer and closer.

He whispered in her ear that he wanted to feel her ass against his body. He pulled out and rolled her over, while simultaneously pulling her hips up to him. He drove his cock into Ava's pussy while his fingers played perfectly with her clit. She could feel his body pounding against her ass, and his cock completely filled her pussy. In moments, they were both screaming out as their bodies exploded in orgasm together. Then they collapsed on the bed, his body covering hers, their breathing deep and synchronized with each other.

As they recovered, the stranger kissed the back of Ava's neck and shoulders. He whispered in her ear about how much he loved her beautiful body and soul. Ava fell off to sleep feeling safe and content under the weight of his body and his warm breath in her ear.

In the morning, Ava awoke expecting to see her stranger in her bed, but she was alone. At first she was confused and wondered if it had all been a dream, but the sweet, slight soreness of her body told her that the stranger had indeed been with her. Ava still did not know who or what her stranger was, but she knew, deep in her heart, he would return to her for as long as she needed him.

Alicia became a Goddess in 2009. Her mission is to inspire and empower women. Athena's allows her to educate and encourage women to embrace and love all parts of themselves. She is the happy mother of two girls.

Part Three

Playing at Work

Getting it on at work—you know you've thought about it. Here are stories of employees getting much-needed bonuses.

Salon Sexcapades By Goddess Monica Holbrook   65

Joe's By Goddess Karen Horn   71

Day After Day By Goddess Rachael Laurie   79

Ideal Retail Experience By Goddess Jamie Winchester   85

Salon Sexcapades

By Goddess Monica Holbrook

Curtis was my hot neighbor whom I'd had many fantasies about and had masturbated to on many occasions. I remember the first time he walked into the hair salon where I was working. The minute I saw him my pulse began to soar, my palms got sweaty, my legs quivered and my pussy immediately began to get wet. I was not the one to cut his hair that time, so it made for an interesting day. My mind wandered frequently to what I wanted to happen if I were to cut his hair.

I did not have to wait long to find out. The next time he came in for a haircut, his regular hair stylist was out. I offered to cut his hair, he said yes, and I put him on the list. He would be the last client of the night. I think my voice cracked when I called his name at his turn. I was so nervous! I was not sure I'd be able to keep my hand steady enough to do a good job on his hair.

I escorted him back to my chair. We had never been formally introduced, so I told him my name and mentioned he lived upstairs in my building. With a huge grin on his face, he told me he was well aware of that fact. I draped him with the styling cape and asked him what he wanted. It took a moment for him to respond. I think he was debating if I meant his hair or something else. I guess my attraction was obvious. I am sure he could feel the heat coming off my body as I pressed close to him, my breasts against his back, as I ran my fingers through his hair.

It was a quiet evening, so almost everyone had gone home already. There were only myself, my boss and Curtis in the salon. My boss had retreated to her office, leaving Curtis and me alone in the hair cutting area.

Our conversation flowed with ease and eventually drifted toward a sexual nature. He began to tell me how much he enjoyed watching me exercise in my skimpy outfits through my living room sliding glass door, and I told him how much I enjoyed seeing him walking by in his skimpy gym shorts. As I continued cutting his hair I began to get even closer to him. I breathed on his neck and in his ears. I could hear his breath catch every time. I could also see that I was having another affect on him. The cape had a visible bump growing under it.

I had to remind myself that my boss was still here, and the entire front of the store is glass. Anyone going by could easily see inside. I suggested to Curtis that he unzip his pants, release his cock from being so confined, and stroke it for me. I had always wanted to see a guy jerk off under the cape. He happily obliged. My pussy was getting wetter by the moment and my nipples were fully erect. They were clearly visible through my white summer tank top. Curtis was thoroughly enjoying the view.

As I neared the end of the cut I had to get in front of him to finish his sideburns. Being very short, I nearly have to climb into my customers' laps. This time I did so a bit more than usual. I leaned forward so Curtis could look down my top. I could now feel his breath on the top of my breasts. I wanted so much for him to lean over, pull my shirt down and take my nipples one at a time into his mouth.

Suddenly, I heard a noise from the office, and I was pulled back to reality. He stopped stroking his cock and I went behind him one last time and ran my fingers through his hair, massaged his neck for a bit and gently tugged on his ears. He moaned maybe a little too loud when I did that.

Quietly, I told Curtis that I had a fantasy about fooling around in the hair salon, and if he was interested he could drive around back and wait for me while my boss and I locked up the salon. After he paid and left, I went to the break room to retrieve my belongings and unlock the back door, so we'd be able to sneak back in. I was nervous my boss would catch me but excited at the same time. I have always gotten wet when I think about getting caught having sex someplace I shouldn't be.

After turning out all the lights, my boss and I left by the front door, said our good nights and parted ways. When I knew she had gone I drove around to the back of the building. As I suspected, Curtis was patiently waiting for me.

After making sure no one would see us from the mattress store next door—they were open for another thirty minutes—I motioned for Curtis to follow me inside. On the way in he pinched my ass. It was easy to find our way around since there were several low lights on to deter potential robbers. We made our way back to my station. It was then that Curtis took me into his arms and kissed me for the first time. It was soft and sweet, but utterly electric! My pulse quickened and my knees went weak. The kiss began to intensify as our bodies got closer. I could feel his hard cock pressing against me. My pussy was aching to feel his manhood inside me. His hands slid behind my head to pull me in for a deeper kiss. Then he suddenly released my head and began to undress me with great urgency. My top was pulled up over my head, exposing my perky breasts to him. With hands shaking

67

he undid my white shorts, one button at a time, pushed them down my legs and helped me step out of them. He then removed my tiny, white, lacy thong and tossed it aside. With me fully nude, standing there only in my sexy wedge sandals, he stood back for a moment to take in the sight of my body.

With a very shaky hoarse voice, he said "Oh my God! You are so beautiful! I have dreamed about your naked body for so long, and now you are here right in front of me. Only you are so much more beautiful than I could have imagined!"

With that he pulled me close for another kiss. If at all possible, his cock was even harder than it was before. He lifted me up and sat me on the counter, pulled my hair styling chair closer, sat down and began to kiss my inner thighs.

My legs were shaking so badly he put them up over his shoulders for support. He went back to slowly teasing me. In between kissing my inner thighs, Curtis would breathe on my pussy. His breath was so hot and inviting. I was not sure I could take much more of that teasing. I wanted to pull his head in to feel his tongue on my most moist spots, but before I could even think about it, he stood up and leaned over me. He kissed me on the lips then made his way down my neck. I shuddered with sheer pleasure. He gently began to lick my right nipple while using his other hand to roll my left nipple around in little circles.

This man had hit all my erogenous zones. My pussy was throbbing between my legs now, and my juice was running down my legs. Sensing my impatience, he licked his way down my body until his tongue was hovering just over my clit. His tongue touched it, and I almost screamed from the intensity. He circled my clit in one direction, and then the other. He licked around my clit, then down between those moist folds. With his left hand he reached up to play with my left nipple. He slowly slid the middle finger of his right hand into my wet slit and pressed lightly on the upper wall. I could feel my muscles beginning to tighten around his finger.

With each lick of his tongue and thrust of his finger, I climbed closer and closer to a mind-blowing orgasm. He could tell I was nearing an orgasm so he began to suck my clit between his teeth. As he plunged his finger in deeper I let go. My orgasm hit with such force that I almost pushed him back, and sent myself off the counter. My legs wrapped tighter around his neck, and I lifted up, my back arched. He kept his mouth firmly planted on my clit and sucked as I rode my orgasm wave after wave. Finally my orgasm subsided, still causing me to visibly twitch. I pulled him up to me, and kissed him passionately, tasting my juices on his lips.

I pulled his shirt up over his head, tossed it aside and unbuttoned his jeans. I lowered them only enough so that I could release his raging hard-on. I slid all the way to the end of the counter and guided his waiting rod of steel into my hot wet pussy. Holding onto the edge of the counter, I leaned back against the mirror. Curtis began to slowly slide into me. After a few strokes, I demand "Fuck me, Curtis! I want it hard and fast!"

He wrapped his hands around my hips and began increasing the speed of his thrusts, pulling almost all the way out each time so he could watch his cock slide back into me.

I could hear how wet I was. I could feel his balls slap my ass with each thrust. My tits were bouncing as he pumped in and out. He warned me that if he did not slow down he was not going to last much longer. I did not care. I wanted to feel his hot cum inside me.

I used all my strength to keep up the pace. I could feel his cock tightening up. I could feel it getting harder. He thrust deeper as I squeezed my PC muscles around him.

"Oh fuck! I am cumming!" he yelled, as he shot his load deep inside me. He rode me until there was nothing left inside him.

Curtis collapsed on me with a huge sigh. Our heartbeats were off the chart, our breathing labored. As we lay there, we heard a noise from the back of the hair salon. We both turned in time to see Michael, the guy who usually closed up the mattress store, leaning against the wall furiously beating himself to an eruptive climax. It seems that when he was exiting the back of his store he heard what sounded like sexual noises. Curiosity made him try our back door. He was pleased to find the door slightly ajar, so he quietly snuck in to make sure all was okay. All was more than okay—it was the hottest sex scene he had ever encountered.

We decided the next time we had a salon sex rendezvous Michael could join in.

Monica has been with Athena's since 2007. She enjoys being able to teach her customers something they never knew. Monica also owns a hair salon, teaches yoga and enjoys time with her husband and daughter.

Joe's

By Goddess Karen Horn

Working late nights was not always my intention, but there were usually a few perks. The tips couldn't get any better, the clientele was generally friendly, minus the occasional mean drunk, and I made more money working twice a week than I had in my 9-5. On the other hand, being short-staffed meant a very long evening with plenty of work after last call in order to close up shop.

Being the head bartender was a great position, but I couldn't keep bartenders if my life depended on it. Maybe I was too much of a hard ass riding my new staff; pushing them to the edge before the first week came to a close. I liked to be in control, keeping the bar meticulously organized to ensure I was on top of every minute detail.

Joe, the owner, had noticed my desire and need to be in control, so he kept himself hands-off except for when it came to hiring. Joe's only forte in this business was finding the most attractive and desirable women and convincing them that they wanted to work for him. How do you think I went from a loan officer to a bartender? Joe. I had processed the loan he took to revamp the joint and make it into the well-know "Joe's." Weekly he'd come to my branch to say hello and to talk business. He knew I was a classy, professional woman, but he was convinced that I was wasting the "fun, young years of my life" sitting behind a desk, pushing papers.

After a few visits I decided to stop into Joe's after work and see what I had helped him create; I was sold. The atmosphere was unforgettable; the locals and regulars were chatty, friendly and protective of the women behind the bar. Decent location, great music and food—why wouldn't I want to work here? My two nights a week turned into a 40-hour work week, benefits, and overtime. I phased out my bank job to become Joe's head bartender and right hand.

Joe's latest hire walked into the bar like she was gliding on air; such a fresh young face and perfect figure. Her gorgeous blond hair was silky and bouncy as she walked toward the bar. Her sun-kissed face and bright, round, blue eyes went perfectly with her adorable rosy pout. I was instantly intrigued. I couldn't look away—her tight, petite body had me feeling aroused and I wanted to place my face between her thighs and taste every bit of sweetness.

"Hiya! I'm Hillary. Are you Kara?" Her musical voice matched her lovely face and I couldn't help but smile back.

"Indeed I am. Nice to meet you, Hillary."

She extended her hand, I embraced her warm hello and began talking shop.

Seven long hours of training and serving booze can really take a toll on one's body. Despite the aching of my loins, the tension in my neck was unbearable. Once the doors were locked I turned to watch Hillary who was wiping down tables. Her tan midriff was exposed and her breasts hung over the table. I could feel myself becoming quite wet.

This sensation, in response to a woman, was a new feeling that I had never experienced before and didn't know how to handle. I'm sure she could feel me staring at her, but I couldn't stop. I kept imagining her fully naked, hair falling over her eyes as she was bent over the tables wiping them down. I pictured her juicy, large breasts swaying, and her nipples rubbing against the hard surface of the table as she reached to the far end.

The vision was almost more than I could endure, but nothing that a few shots couldn't manipulate and put to rest.

"Hey Hill, what's your poison?"

Hillary glanced up at me with a gleam in her eye and began walking towards the bar as I pulled out two fresh shot glasses. "I've always been a whiskey girl. You?"

"Well, to honor our new employee, we'll skip the Jose and enjoy some JD."

I turned to pull the bottle from the top shelf and managed to watch her reflection in the mirror; her eyes were totally focused on me, making my pussy even wetter than it already was. With both glasses filled to the top, we each downed one, clinking our glasses to ease the burn.

"Another?" I asked as her nose crinkled slightly from the strength of the liquor.

"Yeah. I could use another."

Again the glasses were filled and burned our throats as the sweet poison dribbled down into the pits of our stomachs.

"Here. Chase it with this," I said as I handed Hillary a long neck and watched her delicate hand lift the bottle to her mouth.

Her lips looked moist and plump as she drank, and I wanted to instantly taste her lips and caress my tongue against hers. She caught me watching her and I quickly averted my eyes. I began to wipe the counter and act as if I hadn't been fantasizing about wanting to devour her perfect cunt.

Hillary stood up from the bar stool and began to walk to the end of the bar. She made her way around the back to where I was standing. The whole time she was traveling around the bar, her eyes were fixed on me, adding fuel to the fire. I wanted her so badly but couldn't explain where these intense feelings were coming from.

Hillary was now facing me, smiling and staring intently at my lips. She leaned in and softly kissed my jaw line and then moved to my lips. The softness of her lips upon mine sent a spark through my body, awakening every nerve and leaving my panties soaked. I leaned in slightly and kissed her back, feeling her mouth open slightly to welcome my tongue. Our tongues danced and massaged one another and I could feel the intensity building as our kisses became rougher.

Hillary cupped my firm breast in her hand, and I moaned to let her know that I enjoyed her touch. Before I knew what was going on, Hillary had unbuttoned my jeans and migrated her hands into my pants, cradling my pussy. I slightly spread my legs to allow her to feel the wetness she had created. She inserted one finger into my succulent hole and removed it to have a taste. Watching Hillary suck her finger deep into her mouth, close her eyes and moan as if she was in ecstasy threw me into a raging fit of pleasure. I had to rub my clit. Hillary watched me as I manipulated my pussy and screamed out in delight, bringing myself to climax.

"Up on the bar—now!" she commanded then began to force her mouth onto mine and bite my lower lip.

I wasn't used to taking orders but I wanted to be submissive to this amazing goddess. While sliding up onto the bar, I kicked off my shoes and let Hillary take my foot in her hand. She lovingly caressed my bare foot and then began to nibble on my toes. I was new to toes, but watching her stare at me while placing my big toe in her mouth was totally erotic. I could imagine that this was what she would look like if she was sucking on a hard, big cock. After teasing my toes for a bit, Hillary began to tug on my jeans, and I appreciatively lifted my hips while she slid them carefully down to my calves, kissing my knees and massaging my thighs. I let my jeans fall to the floor and hung my legs off the side of the shiny, wooden bar.

"May I?" Hillary asked, as she gestured toward my panties, which by now were soaked with cum.

I opened my legs like I was carefully revealing a gift to her, watching her eyes light up when she pulled my panties to the side to gaze.

"Mmm. Nothing like a clean shaven pussy."

She leaned in to take a taste. Her soft, hot tongue felt so smooth on my nether lips that I was losing control while waiting for her to taste my swollen clit. Once her tongue flicked my clit a few times I could tell that she was going to make me work for what I wanted.

"How bad do you want me, Kara?"

"Mmmm...so bad...so, so bad." I whispered as she kissed my inner thighs and trailed down my leg to my calf. "Please Hillary...suck my pussy and make me cum."

"That's right, Kara, beg for what you want. Tell me how bad I make you ache."

"I've been wet all night since you walked through those door. Please don't make me!"

Then the game began.

Hillary unbuttoned her tight, denim jeans and slowly slid them down to the floor. She stepped out and turned to reveal a voluptuous apple bottom that bounced delicately. The thong she was wearing added to the appeal, and I wanted to lick and bite every inch of it. When she faced me, the playful grin on her face drove me wild and she began to remove her low-cut tank top that sat deliciously on her torso. Her large, tan breasts were encased in a low-cut bra, which cut off just above the nipple and I felt myself becoming more and more eager. Standing in front of me was a goddess, so beautiful and poised yet so sexy and ravenous. Taking a few steps toward me she rested her hands on my thighs and sighed, "Now beg for me, and I promise you will be rewarded."

How could I resist this creature; being forced to beg was cruel and degrading, yet I was enjoying every minute of it.

"Hillary...please. Fuck me. Lick my pussy and pull my hair."

"Mmmm...you like your hair pulled?"

"Yes. Hard."

And with that Hillary grabbed me by the back of my hair, yanked my head back and began to kiss me while rubbing my pussy vigorously.

My hips bucked with delight and I begged her to fuck me. Fuck me hard.

Her hot, moist breath felt incredible while she teased my clit and licked my lips. She plunged her tongue in and out of my deep, wet hole and then trailed down to explore the vast area.

"Hillary! Please! please sit on my face I can't take it any longer."

"I'll tell you when you're going to eat me and I'll tell you when you've had enough!"

Her harsh words made me react with ill manners and I felt my arm extend back and I roughly smacked her ass and grabbed it while she had gone back to fucking me with her tongue. I wanted to be punished, I wanted her to be rough and mainly I wanted her to make me feel dirty. Hillary rose from my crevasse and grabbed the hand that had slapped her.

"Did you like that? Do you like touching me?" she whispered.

With that, she forced my limp hand between her legs and I began to explore her soft, trimmed pussy. I felt the hot wetness dripping from her lips and wanted nothing more than to bury my face in her sweet nectar. I wanted to rise up with hot, glistening juices on my face and show her I loved how she tasted.

"Lay back Kara! Now it's my turn."

I laid my warm back onto the icy bar and watched Hillary quickly remove her tight bra and thong and climb up onto the bar. She straddled me in the 69 position, sitting up on my face. I began to inhale her sweet aroma and I let my tongue have a taste. I enjoyed her lovely pussy so much I had to grip her thighs and pull her deeper onto my mouth. She ground her hips and rubbed her clit against my tongue and lips while I tried to lick her dry, but her wetness was so juicy and constantly replenished. I could feel her thighs tightening as she reached her climax; her erotic cry of pleasure sent chills through my body. We laid there on the bar, panting for air as we were both exhausted with pure satisfaction.

In 2009 Karen became a Goddess to enrich women's lives and help them find their inner vixen. Reading and writing are enjoyable pastimes, and are just two of the creative endeavors that she likes to explore while in bed. She is the mother of three cats, and a loving "wife" to her Bub.

Day After Day

By Goddess Rachael Laurie

With one calloused hand he cupped her supple breast, while the other hand was quickly gyrating over her clitoris to bring her to climax. He gently licked her earlobe sending shivers to her toes. He breathed her name.

"Allison." So soft and sweet.

"Allison." His voice was rougher.

She was so hot and wet, ready to cum with his touch.

"ALLISON!" he yelled.

Allison opened her eyes to see her husband dressed and ready for work, standing over her.

"I don't mind letting you sleep in, but the kids need breakfast, and…"

Allison let him go on about all the things she needed to get done even though she knew perfectly well that he gets up with the kids one day a week before her, and he's an expert. But she was still in shock that she was so close to climax and didn't get to finish that she let him finish. She didn't want to fight today.

Where was the man in her dream? With his hands that knew exactly where to touch and when. Where was the man who would breathe her name just as she was going to climax? Where was the car sex or the floor sex or the foreplay? They went away when her husband Dan got his promotion.

"All the stress," he would say.

"I'm too tired," he would say.

At one point they worked side by side at the printing company. Getting dirty together, taking lunches together, showering together. Now Dan was her boss and had no time for her. It was all about work.

Allison jumped out of bed and got on with her morning routine— kids' breakfast, get dressed, kids to school, off to work. Day after long day.

After dropping everyone off, Allison had a quiet 20-minute drive to work. She couldn't help thinking about her dream. Instantly she was wet. She let one hand come off the steering wheel and slip into her jeans. When she parted her lips she could feel how wet she really was. She let her fingers dip into her center and back out. Playing with her clitoris she realized she might crash. She pulled the car over, put it in park and reached in her purse. She pulled out her always trusty Petals Vibe®. She snuck the purple flower into her jeans and let it penetrate her. The petals rested perfectly on her clit, and she pushed the button. It felt so good. She started to get warm so she turned up the speed. Her hips started to unconsciously move back and forth as she let the flower ease in and out. Her toes were curling.

Knock, knock, knock. Allison jumped and swore hard. Looking up, there was a cop. Without thinking she pulled the vibrator out and shoved it into her purse, then rolled her window down.

"Excuse me, Ma'am. What did you just put in your purse?"

Allison couldn't think straight; she couldn't speak. She reached into her purse and pulled out the flower. Tentatively she held it up. The police officer grinned.

"That's what I thought."

Looking from her vibrator to her ring and back, he leaned down to rest his elbows on her open window. Allison looked at the very attractive cop. He had chiseled cheekbones and some dark scruffy facial hair. His blue eyes looked deep into hers. Allison blushed thinking about how it would feel to run her hands down his hard abs, to wrap her fingers around his even harder shaft. To lick it from base to tip.

"I'll let you in on a secret," he whispered.

Allison snapped back to reality. The gorgeous cop pushed the button on the flower. As it buzzed to life, so did her wet passion. She was aching to be touched.

"If you were mine, you would never need this."

He held the flower out to her. As she reached for it he held her hand in place, massaging the vibrating nubbed tip into her palm. Hot tingles ran through her body. Allison's face was red hot. She still couldn't speak. All she could get out was a small squeak.

"Well, you have a nice day."

He let go of the flower, leaving it sitting in her outstretched palm, threw her a dazzling grin and walked back to his car. Allison turned the vibrator off and shoved it in her purse. She was so frustrated and horny. Her entire body was pulsing. Allison put the car in drive and drove the ten minutes to work. Calling her husband on her cell, she told him she needed to see him right away. Sensing the urgency in her voice, he didn't argue.

"Where do you need me?" he asked.

"In the utility closet downstairs—fast," quickly hanging up the phone before he could resist her.

She went down the hall and opened the surprisingly large and tidy closet. She needed to be touched, her whole body was throbbing. Dan walked in quickly behind her, alarm all over his face. Allison couldn't stop herself. She rushed to him, grabbing his hair to pull him in for a long, hard kiss that he needed and she deserved. He managed to pry her off. He looked directly into her eyes and turned to go. Allison felt defeated. But instead of leaving, Dan locked the door and turned around with a small grin.

He was so good-looking. He always kept in shape. She rushed to him and he to her. They crashed in the middle. Allison grabbed at his belt, struggling a bit with the buckle. She could feel his hard cock only getting harder. Dan swiftly undid her work jeans. He slid his hand down her pants to caress her rear and teased her by stroking his thumb on her hip, while his other hand was massaging her heaving breast. She got his belt out of the way and made quick work dropping his pants to the ground. She loved the feel of his hard smooth penis. She heard his breath catch when she wrapped her hand around him. She stroked his warm cock fast. His breath was getting faster.

"Allison." he whispered.

His fingers gently parted her pussy lips and caressed and circled her wet clitoris. Allison started moving her hips back and forth. She was ready to cum, and Dan knew it. Quickly he retracted his fingers and brought them up to her breast. She pulled her shirt off while Dan swiftly undid her bra. Allison's back started to arch. She had to let go of his throbbing cock to hold on to his toned shoulders. He held both of her breasts in his hands and licked each nipple then sucked at them. It felt so good that Allison stumbled. Her back was at the wall now. Dan got down on his knees and pulled her pants off. He parted her lips to see her pink inside. He licked her gently, up and down circling her clitoris, flicking it with his tongue. Then he entered with his fingers while still licking her up and down.

He stood up and Allison immediately wrapped her legs around him. One small move and his thick hot member penetrated her. She was so wet and tight. Slowly at first he started to move, just a bit at a time, teasing himself—and her. His rigid cock felt so good in her tight pussy both of them were ready to cum. Allison held on tight to her lover's shoulders, digging her nails in. Dan's muscles were wet with sweat.

He looked deep into her eyes, and whispered, "Allison."

That was it. Allison let go. Moaning she released her orgasm to him. She tightened around Dan's member with each wave of pleasure. She felt so good to him, he released too. Both of them moaned into each other's neck, still moving together, in and out. When the last wave was over they fell to the floor, every nerve ending tingling.

They lay there for a half-hour. They both knew they would catch hell at work, but it was worth it. When they stopped shaking, they stood up and got dressed. Dan went to walk out first. Just before he opened the door, he turned to her.

"I missed you." he said and threw her a kiss.

"I've been here the whole time." she said. "I love you."

"Love you too, honey. See you tonight." he whispered.

That night in bed Allison knew she had her Dan back. She knew because he had that same look in his eyes that he used to, years ago. She knew because he slipped into the shower with her and couldn't keep his hands off of her. Licking and sucking on her breast, licking her pink pussy. And she couldn't keep her hands off of him. Stroking his erect penis and sliding it into her warm mouth licking it up the base to the tip, only to take the whole thing back into her mouth, just to hear him lose his breath.

When he jumped into bed with her he had that same look.

"Are you crazy?" Allison asked.

"Crazy for you," Dan replied. "We have a lot of time to make up, my love."

Rachael is a true goddess, and started her business in January of 2010. Doing parties, and bringing excitement to individuals and couples, she always makes time for play. She is a mother of six great kids, and a wife to her loving soul mate.

The Ideal Retail Experience

By Goddess Jamie Winchester

I had been standing in the front of my store, just waiting for a customer to come in. It had been a slow day and I was trying my best to not be bored to tears. You know those days—the never-ending days at work when you have to seek out that extra cup of coffee with an extra pack of sugar just to stay awake. I kept trying to find something to do to occupy my time. I must have hung and re-hung the same three shirts about seventeen times when finally someone walked in.

I was thrilled just to have some one to talk to, until I really looked at him. To say he was tall, dark and handsome would be a cliché, like something you hear in some crappy romance novel. The first thing I noticed about him was his eyes. They burned an intense blue, in contrast to his jet-black hair, and made me wish I could get lost inside them. In fact I must have for a moment because he kind of made this funny face at me, and I realized I had just been standing there staring.

Oh my God! He was talking to me!

"I'm sorry, what did you say?"

I could feel my cheeks turn red with embarrassment. I hadn't heard a word of it! I was just thinking about running my fingers through that black hair.

"It's okay. I was wondering if you could help me. I'm looking for..."

Damn! Stopped listening again.

I smiled and tried to act like I was paying attention while he went on about something or another. All the while I was taking inventory. Starting at the shoulders: broad and muscular and wrapped in a snug blue, vintage T-shirt. His chest and stomach looked nice and tight and I couldn't help but wonder what was going on inside his jeans.

He must have noticed my wandering eyes, because he stopped talking for a moment.

I finally got him set up with some selections and he went to try things on.

I knocked on the dressing room door, partly because I just wanted to talk to him again and partly because that was what we were trained to do. Something about loss prevention. You talk to the customer while they are in the changing room; if they're trying to steal something, they know that you're right there.

"How's everything? Can I get you another size?"

Without saying a word, he whipped open the door and handed me the pair of jeans he had just tried on. "These are a bit tight."

"Well, I can see why!" I stared down at the growing bulge in his maroon boxer briefs with a bit of disbelief. Was this really happening?

I could feel that growing tingle within my own body at the sight of his strong thighs and toned body standing there in front of me.

"This isn't something we usually offer here." I said coyly, as I slipped into the dressing room, closing the door behind me.

He reached over and wrapped one strong arm around my waist, pulling me in close as I pressed my lips against his. So warm and soft. He slid his tongue deep within my mouth and I could feel that enticing bulge start to grow. I pulled away from his lips and began to slowly administer a trail of kisses upon his gorgeous body. Down his sweet neck, across that firm, smooth chest and on to his tight stomach till I was at the forbidden threshold.

I stopped only for a moment to look up and meet his gaze. I could see the anticipation in his eyes and I flashed him such a sweet innocent smile. I'm sure it will be burned into his frontal lobe forever.

Positioned neatly on my knees, I let my finger tips trace, ever so lightly, across his sides and then curled them around the top of his waistband, pressing into his warm flesh. As I pulled down his boxers, I came face to face with a beautiful, fully erect cock! I paused for just a moment to really take him all in before letting my tongue trail tiny circles up and down his shaft. Just smooth and gentle at first. Nice and teasing until he really started to squirm. I finally pressed my lips to the head of his cock and let his whole shaft push deep within my mouth. I heard a little moan escape his lips and then that sigh of complete satisfaction at the moment of penetration.

By now the tingling in my own body had become so much more and I could feel how wet my panties had become. I slid a solitary finger underneath my skirt, pushing my panties aside, and let it glide up and down my slit, making my little body ache with excitement. He must have noticed, because he grabbed my hand and brought my finger up to his mouth, gently licking and sucking off my sweet juices.

He lifted my trembling body up and placed me gently on the small bench in the dressing room, settling himself neatly in front of me on the floor. He placed his big hands on each thigh and I instinctively hiked my skirt up for him. There was no use being shy at this point. His hands rubbed up and down my inner thighs in long, smooth strokes, slowly spreading my thighs further and further apart. My panties were soaked with my sweet pussy juice and I knew things were only going to get wetter!

Leaving my panties in place, he nestled his face in close, allowing me to feel his warm breath on my eager little kitty! He gave my pussy a long warm kiss, so sweet and so tender for a complete chance encounter in a dressing room! Then he started to run his tongue up and down over my hot pink panties making me squirm with delight. He slid those strong hands up to my hips and pulled the strings of my thong down, tossing it to the floor. Finally I could feel him on my bare skin! His warm, soft lips, his wet tongue, gliding up and down my perfect little slit. My pussy began to throb and I grabbed his head and pressed him deep into my honey pot. He began to suck and nibble on my swollen pink clit, sending waves of ecstasy all the way down to my toes.

It was just at this moment that I caught a glimpse of us in the dressing room mirror. There I was, the cute raven-haired college girl. Long toned legs spread wide open, with a gorgeous man's mouth pressed up in between them! Vigorously licking away, covering his face and mouth in my sweet nectar! It was picture perfect!

My breath became shallower and my tiny voice became higher and higher pitched until I was sure I was going to scream out and get caught! I bit down on my bottom lip and just as I was about to explode, he slipped two fingers deep inside me and gave me that "come hither" motion! Ha! Come hither? No problem! With his lips on my clit and his fingers deep inside me, I gushed my hot juices all over him as my body quivered and trembled from head to toe! I closed my eyes and let the waves of passion wash over me while he gently licked up every last drop of my sweet cum.

He looked up and smiled at me, his eyes wild and glistening, eager for more, when there was a knock on the door.

"Everything all right in there, Amber?"

"Uh, ya… I uh…," I stammered, trying to come up with and answer.

"She was just helping me with this zipper," he said. So cool and confident. He saved me.

I grabbed my panties off the floor and stuffed them into my pocket while he threw on those too tight jeans and let me slip out of the dressing room door.

My boss was standing there waiting for me. "Amber" she said, "you know, we usually don't go into the dressing room to help a customer."

"Oh, I know. I'm sorry…he just really…seemed to need my help and…"

"It's fine. Did everything work out?"

"I'd say so."

I couldn't help but let a big smile play across my lips as he walked out of the dressing room. I still didn't even know who "he" was!

He came up to me and smiled again.

"So, Amber was it?"

"Ya…this almost doesn't seem fair! After what you just did for me. I guess I owe you one!"

"No worries." He smiled. "I know where you work."

Jamie Winchester has been a Goddess since 2009 and loves teaching others about sexuality. She has a blast at every party! Jamie is a mother, a lover, a cookie baker, and a girl who loves to celebrate!

Part Four

Once upon a time . . . there was a happy ending.

Waking and Wanting By Goddess Corinne Geary   93

Who Says You Can't Go Home Again By Goddess Jan Simard   99

Picture Perfect By Goddess Jennifer Wilson   107

Le Petit Mort By Goddess Christine Laplante   115

Waking and Wanting

By Goddess Corinne Geary

Venus wakes up to Joseph massaging and caressing her soft, curvaceous body, her supple breasts perky and erect from the touch of his hand on her. While stroking her he feels the passion building as he gently tries to wake her from her peaceful slumber. She's such a beauty, with her chestnut hair falling so perfectly around her face. Lips plump and juicy, ready to kiss. He's anxious to wake her.

She moans and turns toward her lover to reveal the "come fuck me" eyes that drive him wild. Her blue-grey eyes sparkle—he has butterflies. How is it she manages to make him melt with a glance?

She leans in toward Joseph, looking forward to the embrace. Joseph wraps his strong arms around her as if she was made to fit between his broad, meaty shoulders.

Their bodies connect as she begins kissing him with a strength that makes his body stiffen and writhe with pleasure. He pants and gasps. She continues with her electric kisses that jolt him.

He's addicted to her.

She stops kissing him and smiles, for she has a secret. One that Joseph is beginning to discover. She has a power. He doesn't quite understand it, but is eager to learn more. She can melt a man with her body, and is able to arouse intense feelings inside both their bodies. She can play with her energy. She knows why she's here.

Grabbing the bulge he developed, Venus leans in for another kiss and exerts her spark. Joseph moans, overwhelmed by the fire he feels as his body fills with pleasure.

"OH… MY… GOD… I am cuming!" he exclaims.

He writhes and moves as he moans. She keeps sending her passion flowing into his body through their mouths. She opens her mouth and with her tongue, grazes the roof of his mouth, slides over his gums, onto his lips where she gently bites the lower one then quickly kisses away the sting, giving him a variety of sensations in quick succession. She seems to know exactly what to do next.

Joseph doesn't understand how she does it. She has an unlimited bag of tricks.

She moves her kisses from his mouth, with intensity, over his cheek to his ear, licks from his ear down to his neck, where she pauses only a moment. He feels her. His legs tense, and his toes curl up, pointing at the energy she administers with her mouth. Her mouth moves from his neck, down his exposed chest as her tongue gently licks to just above the top of his elegant, silk shorts.

She slips off his shorts, exposing his manliness bulging out of the tight, black boxer briefs.

"God, I love his prick." she thinks. "I can't wait until he slides into me." She loves the way he always shows he's interested.

Quickly removing his sexy underwear, she cups him gently in her hand. She eyes him. He trembles. She makes him tingle. Slowly, she uses her mouth to explore down to his pubic region. She licks that crease of skin between his left leg and his crotch. She breathes with excitement. She looks forward to feeling him in her mouth. She loves his large, thick, hot cock in her mouth. Taking it in and mmmmm… She is looking forward to this as much as he is.

He eagerly anticipates her next moves. She is fucking incredible!

"OHHH, DAMN, VENUS!" he thinks.

Suddenly, she interrupts his thoughts by simultaneously grabbing his testicles with her left hand, the shaft of his penis with her right hand, and the tip of his volcano with her mouth. She circles the tip of him with her tongue, exhaling heavily as her pussy throbs between her legs.

"Here we go." she thinks, and smiles.

She loves doing this to him. She grasps his penis tighter as she makes the descent down his shaft, allowing her hot, mouth juices to drip and combine with his fluids to assist in her endeavor.

As he is being carried away by the combination of her mouth and hands, she's inspired to try new and exciting things since she is rather bored by any routine. Although she expects Joseph to blush afterward, she wants to leave him speechless. Her goal is to leave him paralyzed by her love each time. Her mind races. Sometimes she doesn't know what her next move will be. It just seems to come naturally. She looks up while moving her right hand up his chest, keeping her grasp on his tank.

Those eyes, those…oh my goodness…ahhhhhh…

"How do you do this?" he asks.

She smiles wryly.

Very slowly, as if in slow motion, Venus sucks on his cock up and down while following her mouth with her hand in a twisting motion. She slobbers all over him, loving it wet and sticky. She gradually speeds up. She makes eye contact with him while she sucks him off, something she loves to do. She knows it makes him hot.

She moans as she realizes she is already dripping in her sexy black lace panties. He grabs her ass as if he knew her thoughts, sliding his hands from her ass over her body, down her soft hips and pausing as he cups her forbidden fruit. He can't help himself. He knows one wrong move, and she will take it all away. He decides to just stop there, sit back and wait for her okay.

Venus moves her hand on top of his, flashes those eyes and smiles to let him know to keep going. He loves that she sometimes lets him move forward right away, and sometimes makes him wait. She likes to let it build. He knows she holds the power.

Joseph slides his hand down inside her lace panties, sliding them downward over her sleek legs. She quivers and is turned on by his actions. He is getting hornier by the minute. He wants her womanly body to take him inside. He needs it.

"She's a drug," he thinks, as his eyes roll back.

"With lips like that, this girl is born to suck me off," he muses to himself. Her full luscious lips really know what they are doing. She slides her tongue back and forth all the while keeping her lips pursed over his cock. "The hotter she gets, the better she is," he thinks.

He presses his hands against her legs in an effort to get her to expose her fruit. He admires her body, loving her sexy curves. He slides his hand over her stomach and stops. She trembles. He caresses down to her thighs as he makes her turn toward her pussy, forcing her to stop what she was doing.

She gasps—she loves his mouth on her body. He loves how worked up she gets when she does it to him; he loves them both getting so hot and bothered.

He cradles her thighs in his hands and leans in as he gets ready to feast. He begins to lap slowly from the bottom of her shaved pussy to the top of her clit. He laps up her love as she releases into ecstasy. Venus arches her back as she grabs his head. She loves his feasting on her.

Venus begs Joseph to move up and get inside her. He rises to her level. She kisses him, her juices still on his lips. She feels his cock grazing her leg, making a magnetic turn toward her mate. She moves him between her legs. Joseph's large member is standing at attention, ready to serve, and then he is in her. Slowly, their wet friction is more than either can handle. They moan together as their passion boils. In a world of their own, they gaze into each other's eyes.

"OOOH…Her pussy is so fucking tight!" he thinks, as he rides her body hard.

Venus loves Joseph's hard cock inside her cunt. She loves the feeling of her fingertips on her clit as he fucks her. "Harder!" she screams out all breathy, and he slams his cock harder into her body. The harder he fucks her, the faster her fingers slide over her clit.

He gets off on her hands stroking her own body while he fucks her. He loves the look of excitement in her eyes and the sound of her breathing rhythmically with each of his thrusts. Venus's pussy begins to tighten, her breathing changes, her back arches and she can't help but cum. As she does, he feels her pussy grab hold of his hard cock. Her pussy, her breathing, her erect nipples, her passion spilling on his cock—it's all too much for him to handle. He feels himself getting closer to orgasm. He pounds her cunt faster and harder than ever, loving the virgin-like grip her pussy suddenly has on him. Inhaling the smell of sex that has filled the room, he wants to explode inside of her. He wants to give her all his love.

She calls out to him, "Cum baby, cum inside me, let it go!"

That was all he could handle. Her words act like a fuse on a bomb, his cock ready to burst inside of her. He fills her with his cum. She gets off on the feeling of his cum releasing inside of her.

They stay together, but only for a moment, and kiss softly. Venus slowly rises from the bed as she thanks Joseph for waking her in such a pleasant way.

"Really, the pleasure was all mine," Joseph replied.

Venus smiles, grabs a towel and heads to the shower to get ready. After all, it is Monday morning and they need to head to their respective jobs. Nothing is hotter than fucking before work.

Corinne has been a Goddess since 2005 and enjoys fulfilling her life purpose to help, heal and teach. Corinne is a loving partner and a thriving mother. Corinne gains inspiration for her erotica from her life and her fantasies.

Who Says You Can't Go Home Again

By Goddess Jan Simard

"This sucks!" I completely forgot how hot it is down here in Oklahoma, and I can't believe I got stuck house sitting while my parents travel all over Europe. I left this place as fast as I could seven years ago and hadn't been back since. I grab my bags out of my Jeep and head inside. It was almost dark.

Inside the house it was even hotter; the air conditioning was going to take hours to cool the house down. So I grabbed my bottle of wine and headed out in the backyard where I sat and drank till I didn't mind being back! I had no idea how long I was sitting out there on the patio, but I don't think the temperature dropped one degree.

The cul-de-sac was very quiet. Everyone must vacation all at the same time. "Typical," I said out loud. "Suburbs never change." I took another swig of wine and then I remembered that the neighbors, the Gilmores, had a pool. I know my mother said that they where gone for the summer as well. Wine bottle in hand, I walked over to the fence and unlatched the gate that connected the two yards together. I was sure they wouldn't mind if I used their pool for a little while.

I loved this pool when I was younger. It's an in-ground pool with rock walls built up like a waterfall. We kids used to play Treasure Island in here all summer long. God, that seemed like years ago. They had a son, Justin. I had heard he was some ranch hand cowboy or something. I was trying to think of what he would look like now; he was such a scrawny little kid back then. I couldn't even imagine him being big enough to do the job, let alone get up on a horse!

The water looked so inviting, the moonlight bouncing off the surface. I quickly undressed and dove in. Instant relief. I reached the other side and sat under the waterfall. It was like a soft touch massage running down my back and as I leaned further back and let the water run over my breasts and in between my legs, I opened them a little bit and I started to become aroused.

I lay back all the way on the side of the pool and let the water fall as I massaged my breasts and then slowly let my fingers continue their southern path. "Ohh…umm…" I started to breathe heavier, my fingers moved faster, and then they found their way inside. My heart was pounding and then my body quivered, and shook—so intense!

I rolled over in the water and swam back to where I left my clothes, figuring it has got to be early morning by now. I reached the edge and as I was just about to pull myself out of the water I heard a noise in the yard, and then a man's voice.

"You always did put on a nice show!"

I spun around with a schoolgirl scream to see who was there, only to be met with laughter.

"Ha ha ha! Sorry, I didn't mean to scare you, Sticks." And at that moment I knew exactly who was in the yard with me. Justin was indeed home. He was the only one who ever called me that.

"What are you doing here? And I hate it when you call me that. My name is Stacey." I said trying to find something to cover up with.

"What am I doing here? Last time I checked, this was my house." Justin grabbed a towel from the railing and handed it to me. "And what brings you here, besides trespassing?"

"Oh stop it! Last I heard you were off playing cowboy somewhere. I knew your parents were away, and it was so hot when I drove up, well here I am. And you?" I stepped out of the pool and as quickly as possible I wrapped the towel around my body and scooped up my clothes trying to keep the embarrassment from my face.

"Well, I'm back. The house is now mine. My parents moved down to Florida last year, so instead of spending my entire time at the ranch, I go back and forth. A few days here, and a few days there. You back for good? Is this going to be a nightly thing? If so, I'll need to rearrange some plans."

"You wish! You are such a jerk. Good night!" I made my way back to my yard, not believing what had just happened! I was not going to be able to face him all summer!

I tried to go to sleep, but all I kept thinking about was Justin. He was no longer that scrawny kid I remembered. He had to be at least six feet tall and oh so beautiful, almost God-like! Bronzed skin and deep green eyes. How in the world am I going to see him tomorrow? Dawn came and I heard a car door slam. I got to the window in time to see Justin throw his gear into the back of his pickup truck and take off. At least I won't have to worry about running into him for a while. I fell back into bed with Justin in my head.

It was noon when I finally woke up and jumped into the shower. It was already hot and humid outside, completely miserable. I threw on my little orange sundress to try to stay as cool as possible. I had no idea what I was going to do with myself for the entire summer. My mind quickly replayed the events of the night before. I couldn't believe what had happened! How much wine did I drink to not notice him in the backyard or to hear him walk out there. "What an ass! Why couldn't he have said something before I undressed and got in the pool? Not even a hello! And then to stand there and watch…"

All of a sudden, just thinking about it, I was all excited. It was like my body was betraying me. I'm mad, not aroused!

The day dragged on and finally it was getting dark, which hopefully meant it would cool down a little bit. I grabbed a bottle of water and headed out to the back patio. I was lounging out there for a while before I saw an envelope on the table with "Sticks" written on it. I picked it up and looked around and wondered when the letter was dropped off. Inside the note it read, 'Dinner at 8pm.' I flipped it over and it said nothing else. I was intrigued. I went into the house and grabbed another bottle of wine and started to walk next door. Nothing else to do…

I tapped on the back kitchen door and was greeted by a sassy grin, "Didn't think you were coming over."

"I was curious to see what you were cooking." I walked under his arm to get inside, "Got a corkscrew?"

He laughed as he closed the door, "Sticks, you haven't changed a bit!"

We ate pizza in the living room while we caught up on each other's lives. He was fascinating! He was definitely not the boy I remembered.

He was all man and I felt myself getting hotter thinking about him. His big strong hands, his gorgeous body, and then an image of him completely naked sprang into my mind and I got even more aroused!

"Are you okay? You look flushed." he asked.

I jumped out of my thoughts. "Oh, I'm fine, just a little hot."

"Feel like doing a little swimming?"

"I didn't bring my suit." I felt my checks get red. Justin leaned over me, grabbed my wine glass and placed it on the table. "It's ok, I don't have mine either." And with that he gently came closer and kissed me. A bolt of electricity shot through my body. We stood up and headed for the pool.

Before I knew it, he was naked and already in the pool.

"What are you waiting for?"

"Turn around!"

"Why?"

"Just do it, or I'll leave!" I said with a grin. With a smile he turned around and I let my dress and panties fall to the ground, all in one fell swoop.

I stepped into the pool and he turned around, "Now was that so bad?"

"Nooooo." I teased.

In an instant, I was in his arms. He kissed me and let his tongue tease my lips for just an instant. His hands were on my back, holding me tight. He traced my jaw line with his mouth, tasting as he kissed my neck and then went lower to caress my breasts. He sucked in one nipple, and then moved over and nibbled the other. His touch was like fire and ice!

He picked me up and placed me on the side of the pool where his mouth continued its journey exploring my chest and then slowly going down…ribs…stomach…his hands brushed my thighs as I opened up and he went down even further. I have never felt anything like this before, quivering, shaking as his mouth went further down until he found what it was craving.

Slowly he kissed my inner thigh and with each kiss, as he got closer, my legs opened even wider until finally he found my hidden desires!

He teased my clitoris. Excitement ripped through my body. He parted my lips and tasted my sweet juice as I moaned and arched my back. His tongue and his hands licked and caressed until my body pulsed and pumped with excitement! I came right there—my body shaking. He stopped and jumped out of the pool and for the first time, I saw him completely naked. He was breathtaking! He got down and lay on top of me and slowly entered my body. He thrust his penis deep inside me, his speed got faster, then deeper, and then faster again. I came again, my body pulsing against his. I couldn't get any closer to him, and I wanted more.

I told him to roll over and I got on top, kissing his mouth and slowly making my way down to his giant member. I licked, and I sucked and then took his penis in my mouth, sucking and teasing. I could feel his body getting hotter and his moans were getting louder, but I wasn't quite ready to be done yet.

I moved up and straddled his penis, sitting up and facing him. I took all of him in. And while he lay there watching me, I took my left hand and starting touching myself. Rubbing, teasing…faster and faster while my other hand rubbed and played with my breasts! And I could feel his excitement inside me while he watched me touch myself. He couldn't handle any more waiting…he lifted me off of him and got behind me. I was on all fours and he entered me. I screamed with excitement. He reached out and grabbed a handful of hair and that put me right over the edge! My body pulsed and released again but this time it was so intense as I kept pushing myself harder into him.

With one last thrust and a deep moan, we finished together and dropped to the ground from pure exhaustion!

"Oh my God!" was all I could say as we rolled over to lie in each other's arms.

"When I saw you last night, it took all my restraint not to come over and ravage you right then and there," Justin whispered in my ear.

I smiled and nuzzled more into him. What an incredible man. This is going to be one hell of a summer!

Janette has been a Goddess since 2005 and loves doing parties. Her life purpose is to educate adults on how much fun their relationships and their bedrooms can be. Every day, take a step out of your comfort zone and see all the great things that come your way. She is a loving wife, a caring mother and a passionate lover.

Picture Perfect

By Goddess Jennifer Wilson

Kendra patiently waited at the table as she intently looked at her husband's newest photos. One by one she flipped through the black and whites, studying every detail. She took a deep breath, removed her glasses and pinched the bridge of her nose. A few strands of her long brown hair fell into her face as she listened to the evening rain calmly tap the darkened skylight above.

"Are you ready to order or are we waiting for someone?"

Kendra, startled, looked up to see a tall, thin, tan woman dressed in all black, with a long white apron, staring back at her. She noticed the waitresses straight black hair simply pulled into a pony tail, but still so attractive. Her make-up was light, and worn in just the right way. Kendra imagined photographing this woman at a beach or maybe on an old bridge over a small river. The waitress smiled a soft elegant, yet very warm, smile and repeated, "Are you expecting someone else?"

Kendra glanced at the door then back at the waitress,

"I'm waiting for my friend. Today's her birthday."

The waitress leaned over Kendra to grab the dessert menu. Kendra took a deep breath of the waitress's perfume.

"Why don't you pick something out for dessert and we can surprise her."

Kendra checked the door once again and pointed to a white truffle and raspberry cheesecake.

"This is her favorite. We'll need two forks with it. And can you bring us a bottle of your house cabernet?"

The waitress gave that same warm smile as she nodded and walked away.

Kendra began collecting the photos once again when she heard a familiar voice.

"Hey Ken, sorry I'm late."

Kendra immediately noticed the exquisite perfume Desiree always wore. She looked up with excitement to see her best friend of twenty years. Desiree glanced at the menu as she put her new red Prada® purse down in the booth and slowly untied and removed her long tan trench coat.

"I stepped in a big puddle as I was walking in and got my new shoes all wet."

Desiree lifted her leg to show off her slim red heels that matched her purse.

"Brian got them for me for my birthday—he just doesn't know it. Gotta love riding that alimony pony."

Desiree laughed as she slid into the booth. Kendra chuckled as she reached into her purse. She pulled out a square gift, wrapped in purple paper with a black bow. A shiny silver "30" hung from the knot of the bow.

"Oh, Ken. I told you not to! Dinner is fine."

"Just open it. It's part one of your gift."

Desiree carefully pulled the paper off as so not to disturb her perfectly French-manicured nails. Her eyes teared immediately as she looked at the cover that said, "Here's to the past." She flipped the book open to see old pictures of her and Kendra over the past twenty years.

"Oh man, this seems like a lifetime ago. Look at how goofy we looked. Our lives before highlights and manicures."

"And your fake boobs." Kendra laughed.

They heard a woman chuckle as they looked up to see the waitress standing at the table with their bottle of wine. The waitress poured their drinks and took their orders. Kendra raised her glass and cleared her throat with a soft cough.

"Now for the next portion of your photo album—the present. After dinner we are going to the studio and Jason is going to take some pictures to add to your album."

Desiree smiled excitedly. "It will be like that time we pretended we were professional models. You always told me I would be a model by the time I was 30. Now it's true."

"I think it will be so much fun. Is there anything else you wanted for your birthday?"

Desiree let out a small sigh as she raised her glass.

"I just want to live. You know, do something I've never done before. I just don't want to be old. I guess with being thirty and newly divorced, I feel like I am getting another chance at life and I'm gonna live it!"

The girls clinked their glasses and drank as the waitress put their perfectly prepared Italian meals in front of them. The two reminisced about times past as they worked through the bottle of wine and ate. Soon the entire wait staff was singing "Happy Birthday" over a huge slice of white truffle raspberry cheesecake.

After dinner the two found themselves crouched in a small, dark doorway hiding from the rain. Desiree held a small umbrella over herself and Kendra while Kendra fumbled in her purse for the keys. Soon a "Picture Perfect Photography" sign lit up in the window followed by the sound of a deadbolt being disengaged. A tall, thin casually dressed man opened the door. He smiled warmly at the women.

"Finally, the models I ordered."

The girls giggled. Kendra stepped through the door and gave the man a kiss. Desiree followed her in.

"What, no kiss?" he laughed.

"I haven't had THAT much to drink." Desiree teased back.

The girls walked into the brightly lit studio while Jason secured the door once again. Kendra removed her grey knit sweater and watched Desiree as she, once again, slowly removed her long trench coat. She wondered how something so simple could look so beautiful. Desiree walked over to Kendra and removed the clip from Kendra's hair.

"It's my modeling session and I want you to show off those beautiful brown locks you have."

Kendra ran her hand through her hair and nodded at Desiree.

"Okay girls, it's modeling time." Jason announced as he adjusted the large umbrella lights on either side of the long white drapes that hung loosely from the ceiling covering the hard concrete floor.

"Why don't we start with Kendra sitting facing the left and Desiree you sit back to back with her."

The girls giggled as they flung their hair and made faces at Jason. The flashes of light seemed to come at a steady pace as Jason encouraged the girls to have fun with the camera.

"Okay, why don't we take some more serious pictures now." Jason suggested, as he adjusted the settings on his camera.

Kendra sat on the white drapes as Desiree sat behind her and wrapped her arms around Kendra. The girls began giggling again.

"Come on ladies, serious and sexy," Jason encouraged.

The girls both took a deep breath trying to oblige Jason's request. More flashes of light. Desiree adjusted her position. Her hand softly grazed Kendra's inner thigh. Kendra quickly realized she liked the feeling of Desiree's touch. She looked back at her friend and gave her a soft, welcoming smile. Desiree nervously giggled and blushed. Kendra found her reaction stimulating and wondered if this is what Desiree meant by "living life." The girls changed positions again. Desiree was lying on her side and Kendra was positioned behind her. This time the girls were quieter, both feeling a new and exciting connection they had never felt before. As the flashes of light continued, Kendra began to softly tickle the small of Desiree's back.

"Okay, ladies. Now some with you two facing each other." Jason suggested as he began adjusting his camera once again. The girls faced each other and stared expressionless into each other's eyes. Kendra felt more excited as she moved closer to Desiree and saw her erect nipples. Desiree reached out and firmly grasped Kendra's hips, pulling Kendra closer to her. Thrown off balance, Kendra fell towards her. The girls began giggling once again.

"Sorry, I guess I don't know my own strength." Desiree laughed nervously.

As Kendra began to reposition herself she felt a rush of excitement as Desiree's stiff nipples brushed against hers. Without any thought, Kendra leaned over and softly kissed Desiree. Discomfited, Kendra pulled back quickly. She stumbled for words, but before she could say anything, Desiree ran her hands through Kendra's hair and pulled her close. She began to passionately kiss Kendra.

Jason slowly lowered the camera to better take in the girls kissing seductively. Kendra slowly moved her hands into Desiree's low cut shirt to feel her erect nipples. Desiree let out a soft moan as she moved her lips down Kendra's neck and began to remove Kendra's shirt. Jason felt his penis begin to swell, but did not want to disturb the girls. He placed his camera on a shelf filled with camera equipment. He picked up a movie camera and set it on a tripod. The girls were now topless and exploring each other's nipples with their mouths. Desiree moved her hands up Kendra's skirt and pulled down her black thong panties. As Kendra slowly began to lie down, she gently guided Desiree by the back of the neck towards her.

"I want to feel more of your tongue." she whispered in Desiree's ear and softly kissed her again. Desiree pulled Kendra's skirt up and gently spread her knees apart. She began to tenderly lick Kendra's soft, shaved, wet pussy. Kendra let out a moan and began to move her hips back and forth. She looked toward Jason, who was now fully erect, and indicated for him to come to her. As Jason began to walk towards Kendra, she directed him to Desiree. Jason moved behind Desiree and slowly lifted her skirt up. To his pleasure he discovered Desiree was not wearing panties and was incredibly wet. He undid his pants and slid them off. He took a moment to caress Desiree's soft bottom before he slowly slid himself inside her.

Jason felt Desiree push herself back towards him. He felt every inch of her soft wet pussy around his engorged shaft. He watched his wife's face as she experienced the pleasure of feeling her best friend licking inside her. Jason took Desiree by the hips and began thrusting harder and harder into her. The sound of the rain on the windows could barely be heard with the moaning coming from Kendra. Desiree lifted her head to look Kendra in the eyes as she slid her fingers into her, affectionately licking Kendra's energized clitoris.

Kendra softly moved Desiree's head up as she began to change positions. She began kissing Desiree passionately as Jason slid his swollen penis out of Desiree. He laid back on the floor and told the girls to come to him. Kendra straddled her husband and let out a loud moan as his hard cock pushed into her. Desiree positioned herself over his mouth while facing Kendra. The two began kissing each other's breasts and lips. They both powerfully yet softly explored one another's bodies. Desiree rocked her hips as Jason shoved his tongue inside her, moaning louder and rocking harder. Jason slid his finger inside her asshole as he continued to rapidly move his tongue around her pulsating pussy. Hearing Desiree's sounds of complete pleasure, Kendra began kissing her harder as she ground her pussy into her husband, getting every inch of him inside her. Suddenly she felt Desiree stiffen as she let out a screaming moan. The sound of her friend's pleasure made Kendra's clitoris explode with excitement. Jason could not hold it back any longer. The sound of the two women in ecstasy made him blow everything he could into his wife.

The three laid together for the rest of the night kissing and softly touching each other until they all fell asleep. A week later Desiree opened her mailbox to find a video and a note that read, "Here's your Picture Perfect birthday. Can't wait for next year." Desiree smiled and immediately went inside to relive the night.

Jennifer has been a Goddess since February, 2010. Her goal is to educate and encourage men and women to enhance their sexual experiences. She and her husband adore their three children and two stepchildren.

Le Petit Mort

By Goddess Christine Laplante

She stirred in the bed next to me, her body wrapped around mine, holding tightly. She smelled sweet, her skin soft and smooth. I couldn't help but run my hand down her thigh, to feel the tender skin under my hand, the round of her ass kissing my palm. It took all the restraint I had not to squeeze her into me as I was already beginning to swell.

She rolled slightly, with a half-sleep moan that hit me in my core and shot a tingle right between my legs. Resolve was waning and I knew that soon I would need to taste her. The morning dew of her cunt, resting on the well-tended mound of hair wafting the musk of her in my direction was seductive. It was alluring, drawing me towards her, beckoning me inside of her.

I moved, re-positioning myself, and she grabbed fiercely. "Don't worry." I whispered. "I am not going anywhere."

"Mmmm," was her reply as she now lay on her back, my mouth kissing her stomach, the crest above her pubis, the tuft of hair at the triangle marking the beginning of her holy place. A small kiss on her already wet crevice of delight, then I moved to her thigh. She opened for me further, moaning again, and I could smell her heat. I opened my mouth wide, biting and sucking just inside her leg, drawing the muscle into my mouth enough to feel good, not enough to hurt. Having woken up the nerves in one leg, I grazed over her cunt with a breath, and moved to the other side. Sucking, biting, drawing her into me as I felt her rise to try and touch me, to move me to the center that was growing hotter and wetter by the second. She would get her way. She knew it, because I couldn't resist. Now it was a waiting game, to see how long I could hold out before I penetrated her.

She was awake now, though her eyes were still closed and I knew she rode that space between dream and morning. Her body moved with my touch. Her cunt swelled with each bite. The heat was unbearable near my face as I stroked her legs. I reached my hands up to touch her stomach, to run my fingers under her breasts, the warmth of the soft underbelly of her welcoming my touch. I reached further and cupped her breasts, slowly making my way to her nipples. She placed her hands over mine and squeezed hard. Restraint had gone with the moan, and I could no longer put off the delicious warmth of her juices.

With ferocity, I placed my mouth over her cunt, sticking my tongue into her wetness, slowly circling her opening. Her slickness welcomed me, pulled me in. My tongue found its way to the tip of her clit and made its way around and around and around again in slow, tender, teasing gyres. My teeth grazed her, and I sucked gently on her clit, drawing it out, pleasing it, worshipping it. She lifted her hips to meet me, forcing herself into my mouth further, cutting off the supply of air to my nose, but I didn't care. I could die here and be perfectly happy.

But not yet, I thought. I'm not done. Forcing myself to live, I lifted my nose so my mouth and tongue played with the center of the universe and my chin put pressure on the opening of her cunt. I knew this

116

would wake her up fully—her nerves, her labia, her cunt all swollen now, juicy, and red with blood flow.

Still licking, kissing, sucking and working her with my mouth, I stuck my fingers inside of her and reached for the spot I knew would put her over the edge. Awake now, she rocked and writhed with each stroke as I drew the blood into her swollen pussy from all angles. Working my fingers, she told me what she wanted with her body. Her moans grew louder and longer. She began to shut me out as all of her became totally engorged. I forced myself in, over and over, until her moan became a slight scream, elongated with breath and pulse. Her cunt, releasing more juice, vibrated with her orgasm. I suckled her a little longer, delighting in the pulse of release.

Then I moved my mouth from her delicious womanhood, and while keeping my hand inside her, I lay my body on top of her. I used my body to fuck her, riding her now while my hand remained inside. My mouth met hers, eager, and I kissed her with her juices still in my mouth. She opened her eyes to look at me, pleading me to let her go again, to continue this ride, and I smiled.

"Where's your Celebrator®?" I asked.

"You want to kill me?" She replied.

"Well, seeing as you almost suffocated me, I figured I would return the favor," I said and smirked.

And out came the Celebrator from the side of her bed. Her already swollen cunt was ready and willing to go to a different place, a higher place, a more intense place. My hand, still inside of her, felt the reaction to the buzz of the Celebrator before it even found its home between her legs. I played with her, turning it on, off, on again. I could feel her eagerness, even though she feigned death. My hands were home, my fingers on her trigger, and the one on the Celebrator, anticipating the waterfall of juices about to release from her. I smiled. She winced playfully.

I placed the Celebrator near her clit and drew it forward on her cunt, my fingers resting with pressure just inside her—not far—on the elusive beginning of the tube of tissue that would soon shower me with her ejaculation. She jumped a bit at the sudden orgasm. Her scream was no longer soft, but a full release of energy. But I was not done, by any means. I wanted to keep her there, in orgasm, for as long as she could take it.

I did not let her come down, but rather continued to press at the very crest of her opening, the very top on a small mound of ever-moving tissue, a trigger that I had to constantly find. I was skilled, though, and had run this race before and I was not going to let it elude me, not while I had the grace of her in my hands. She trusted me and I was going to make sure she had the grandest orgasm. As her scream heightened, elongated already, her juices released, a fierce gush of amrita—life juice—spilling forth onto me. Her screams continued as I did not stop there. Her body tried to suffocate my hand, but I was not giving up. I pushed my way inside again to make a slow draw towards the front of her. The Celebrator dancing on her clit, she screamed loudly again as another gush came forth. And another peak, and another pulse, and another push as she released continuously. Her whole body tightened now, tensed as if her brain could take no more ecstasy, and I pushed her just a little further. The scream she had been vocalizing for quite some time now, reaching an even higher pitch as her voice began to give, was part of the grand finale, the fireworks at the end of the show. And the release heightened as the spray from her pussy could not be contained, her whole body pulsed with orgasm, with spasm, with release. And she died—le petit mort.

I turned off the Celebrator and lay it aside. I placed my hands over her labia and gently cupped them closed. I kissed her pubis and blew into my hands, sealing the energy then curled up beside her. "Good morning, beautiful." I whispered.

Christine has been a Goddess since Valentine's Day 2004 and is a member of the Athena's Training Team. Christine's passion is education, especially when it comes to increasing pleasure. Christine frequently teaches sexual integration workshops with her husband, "O."

Part Five

Graphic Novel

These stories are so deliciously descriptive—a feast for the senses. You'll feel the steam of the shower, taste the wine, and hear the roar of the crowd.

Giggles By Goddess Mary Brown   123
Chinese Food By Goddess Amanda Burden   131
All The Discomforts of Home By Goddess Maggie Russell   139
Lipstick By Goddess Christine Reid   143

Giggles

By Goddess Mary Brown

The three girls passed me in the hall, giggling, their books clutched tight against their firm breasts. They had the polished tan look of the "popular" girls—you know, ones who look strangely like a clothing ad? Only they are right in front of you, condemning you with their eyes.

I looked down at my scuffed shoes and my older sister's jeans.

"You should be grateful you can even attend college," rang my mother's words, admonishing me.

I was grateful, I thought stubbornly. It just sucked that I had to give up most of my weeknights and weekends to work at the laundry room, while juggling six courses and staying on a budget that barely covered my college student staples—Ramen noodles, peanut butter and one pack of cheap cigarettes per week.

Instead of gaining the freshmen 15, I had lost about 10 pounds since starting school a few months ago. Actually this was great, since my newly slimmed body fit better in the jeans my sister had given me, once she decided the wardrobe she owned did not fit into her new jet-setting life.

I shrugged, hooked my book bag over my shoulder and started toward my dorm room, hoping my roommate would be out so I wouldn't have to listen to her incessant chatter.

Our dorm room was large and airy and I sighed with relief when I noticed the note on the mirror.

"With Jeff. Be back ???? XOXOXOXO Cherry."

Her real name was Cheryl, but she insisted we all refer to her as Cherry, because of her flaming red hair.

I wondered secretly if there was another reason. Considering all the times she snuck back in the room in the wee hours of the morning, I was pretty sure there was no longer a cherry!

I giggled to myself and then stopped, peering at my face in the mirror. A girl with long, dark, full hair, parted in the middle, and soulful large brown eyes, peered back at me. I was tall, usually towering over the cute, preppy blonds that men seemed to adore. My T-shirt said "I'm Irish, kiss me!" with a leprechaun drinking a beer, left over from some bar offering swag as a way to get their patrons to drink more. At least I filled it out nicely.

I had about three hours before I had to be back for the night shift and decided I would treat myself to a nice hot shower, knowing most of the dorm would be engrossed in Oprah in about five minutes. I stripped, wrapped myself in a tattered old terrycloth robe, grabbed my shower kit and headed down the hall. The bathroom was deserted. I entered the large multi-shower area, set my basket down and slipped out of my robe. I turned on the water, letting it's warmth run down my tired muscles. I closed my eyes and relaxed.

I heard the bathroom door and opened my eyes. No biggie, I thought. We had all become quite accustomed to random females showering in the same vicinity.

"Oh, hi."

The girl who entered the large shower room was one of those blond, preppy ones. I murmured hello, feeling suddenly large and gawky. She slipped off her little, silky, yellow robe, and walked her perfect body over to the showerhead closest to mine. I realized I was staring when she turned and gave me a little smile. I scrubbed at my hair, secretly beating myself up for openly admiring her firm little breasts and tight, tan body.

"You have beautiful breasts, you know," she said.

I heard her voice echo a bit in the room. I blinked suds out of my eyes, trying to focus on the blurred vision in front of me.

"Thanks," I managed to sputter.

She giggled and playfully sudsed up her own pert breasts, knowing I was watching.

"I love breasts," she mouthed silently, as she ran her hands up and down her own.

I knew I was probably standing there with my mouth wide open. I couldn't think of anything to say. I was entranced by her small hands stroking up and down her rosy nipples, the bubbles trailing down her flat, tan belly, the sparkle of the belly button ring flashing and…

I swallowed nervously. She was completely shaved! She must have noticed me looking.

"I think everyone should be shaved. Don't you?" she asked.

I must have looked embarrassed, because she reached over and put her hand on my arm. I looked down into these startling blue eyes and inviting rosy lips.

"I can help you," she offered.

"I, ah, well…" I stuttered.

Why not? I thought to myself. Why the hell not! I had never felt such attraction for a woman, but this arch nemesis of mine was quite appealing. I smiled.

"Sure…"

Let's see what happens, I decided. She reached out a soapy finger to touch one of my always-excited nipples.

"You have the most gorgeous nipples I have ever seen!"

She leaned over a bit and with her tongue tickled the area she had just touched.

Desire coursed through my body.

"Let's get started," she purred, pulling her tongue back away from my throbbing nipple.

"Come and sit here," she said, as she patted the wet plastic seat for the handicapped shower.

Armed with my razor and a bottle of Coochy Crème®, I sat myself down on the seat and looked up at her glorious nakedness. The room was filled with warm steam, and she turned on the handicapped shower detachable showerhead. She knelt before me with it in her hands, smiling wickedly. Her blond curls were plastered wetly to her head. Rivers of water ran down her slim back. She slid a hand between my legs. I willingly opened them, feeling pulsating throbs in my pussy as her hand got closer to my well-trimmed pubic area. She stroked my lips and I leaned back, opening my legs wider, wanting more of her touch.

I felt the coolness of the lotion covering my pubic area as she gently applied the cream. I was completely exposed to her stroking fingers. I kept myself still as the razor made quick work of the dark coarse hair covering me. She pulled the skin tight at my lips, a quiet singsong hum coming from her lips. I dared to place a hand on her head, running my fingers along her wet hair. She leaned back on her heels.

"There! Fantastic!" She gave me a broad smile and put the razor down. "I just need to rinse you."

She aimed the showerhead at my pussy, and turned the dial to a pulsating massage.

"Oooooo!" I exclaimed as the warm water hit my clit, bringing intense pleasure.

She straddled me on the seat, keeping the shower aimed down at my recently shaved pussy. Her breasts hung in my face, begging for my mouth. I flicked my tongue up and down over one nipple while my other hand groped her other breast. The water still pulsed between my legs as she ran her hands over my breasts, pinching the dark red nipples. She moaned while I suckled her breast. I could feel my clit getting hard as the stream of water continued to flow.

She slipped off my lap, pushing my legs open wider, the showerhead now held down under her. She moaned as I scooted forward, my pussy inches from her face. She slipped a finger in. I was so wet, it slid in easily. I wanted to experience this touch—this gentle, naughty touch from her.

I pulled her head closer, becoming bold in my passion. Her finger stroked inside me, touching my most intimate parts. I let out a gasp as her tongue danced around my hard clit. She pushed back the hood and took the whole clit in her mouth, sucking greedily. It was intense! My legs shook and her finger probed deeper. She made small sucking noises as she moaned, the showerhead moving in between her legs.

Time seemed to slow down in that hot steamy shower. Her perfect mouth quivered against me. As she pulled back she huskily whispered, "Baby, baby, I'm cumming!"

She let out an explosive moan and leaned back as she aimed the showerhead at her own smooth pussy. I knelt down next to her and pushed her hand out of the way, dipping my head down, allowing my tongue to lap at her hard clit.

She came in waves as I held her close to my mouth, feeling the sweet nectar release from her delicious kitty. She shuddered as I licked every sensitive inch of her.

"Stop. Wait, wait," she said softly, and stroked my head as I lay my cheek against her belly, still feeling the pulsing waves running through her.

She pulled me up to her, and we kissed slowly, hotly, our tongues intertwining. Her hands reached down, rubbing my clit as the showerhead sprayed against the wall.

"I want to make you cum," she whispered.

She continued to rub my clit with her two fingers, around and around in circles, as she kissed my mouth. Our legs wrapped around each other; I felt her nipple brushing mine. She kept rubbing and our tongues kept tangling playfully. My hips rose up, and I moaned. She responded by rubbing me harder.

"Oh…Yes! Yes! Yes!" I cried.

My head went back as I felt the orgasm build deep in me.

"Do it, cum for me baby," she whispered fiercely, moving her hands around in circles.

"Ooooh, God, don't stop!" I begged.

I came hard, shaking, her hand still stroking my firm clit. Again and again, the waves pulsed through me, feeling such strong contractions deep inside. She kept stroking and before I knew it, I rode another wave and came crashing down hard again, my hips bouncing against her hand.

Her head was bent over my breast, biting and sucking as she pulled the most intense orgasm out of me. "Oh Gooooooooodddddddd."

I breathed in deep, pushing through another earth-shattering orgasm.

"Ai ai ai ah!"

My sounds were primal, tailing off into a whimper as she finally allowed her hand to rest and leaned up to look at me, her blue eyes softened with passion.

"Wow." I finally found my voice.

"Yes, wow," she said as she giggled.

I sat up, and she leaned against me. We both sighed, knowing we should probably get out of the bathroom soon. She stood up, giving me her hand to pull me up on my shaking legs. We clung together for a moment, our wet bodies making a sucking sound as we pulled apart.

I shut off the water, leaving the detachable showerhead where it was, as a sign of defiance—look what we did! She turned off the other shower, wrapped a towel around herself, handed me my robe and kissed me softly on my lips.

I smiled and picked up my kit, and turned to follow her out of the bathroom. She went down the hall, entered her room, turned and blew me a kiss. I caught her kiss and grinned.

As I entered my room, it dawned on me. I hadn't even gotten her name.

Mary has been a goddess since 2005. She enjoys educating women and men about the benefits of a healthy sex life. Her greatest joys in life are her 18-year-old twin daughters, Lauren and Madeline.

Chinese Food

By Goddess Amanda Burden

Deep breath. Check.

Fake smile. Check.

I reach up and before I can knock the door swings open. A pretty young woman bursts out, throws her arms around me, plants a big wet kiss on my cheek and smiles up at me. A tall muscular man steps out behind her.

"Alyssa!" he exclaims, favoring me with a big hug of his own.

"We've missed you so much!"

Finally someone missed me. I stretch my smile a little further.

"Jason. Maggie."

My face feels like it's going to break from smiling.

"I've missed you, too!"

We cross the threshold into a house as familiar to me as my own.

"Where's your new boyfriend?" Maggie asks. "I thought we were going to double date?"

Fresh humiliation washes over me. "He never showed up." I mumble.

Maggie and Jason exchange a knowing look. It always seems like my dates never show up.

"How about this, I'll drive into town and get us some take-out and another bottle of wine." Jason to the rescue, as usual.

"We'll order some Chinese and toast to your freedom from the jackass."

"Actually, why don't I go?" Maggie pipes up from her perch on the counter. "I need to spin by the drugstore anyway and Alyssa looks like she could use one of your fantastic massages!"

I watch in shock as she hops off the counter, grabs her purse, and gives Jason a peck on the cheek.

"I should only be an hour or two."

I feel as if my jaw is lying on the floor in front of me. I can't believe she's being so nice about it! She had to be tired of my parade of boyfriends by now.

"Are you sure you don't mind?" Jason asks with a knowing smile in my direction. "Just get what you used to in college."

College had been so much easier, Maggie had always been with Jason and the three of us would have Chinese food every weekend and watch movies. They were really my best friends, despite my jealousy and all the nasty thoughts I had about her from time to time.

I mope over to the bar and pour myself a big glass of wine, which Jason promptly plucks from my hand.

"I thought you needed a back rub?"

I hesitantly follow him to the couch and sit next to him. He reaches over and places the glass on a table behind me, sweeping my hair back off my face in the same movement. His eyes never leave my gaze.

Could this be the moment I've been waiting for? Is he leaving my best friend for me?

All of my thoughts are swept away as his lips find mine. Our bodies press together. His hands move under my sweater in a moment, cupping my breasts through the thin lace of my bra. I lean back as he presses urgently against me.

I yank off my top. His lips move downward, kissing and sucking every inch of my skin. His hands slide down my body to the thin fabric of my skirt. His lips graze across one of my nipples. I moan in pleasure, arching my back and grinding my hips upward into him. I reach down and pull off his shirt tossing it behind me, knocking the glass of wine down onto my head.

Jason pulls away, laughing at my wine drenched form. Humiliation burns. I reach for something to cover myself. Before I can find anything, he stands and sweeps me up in his arms in one fluid motion.

"I can't have you dripping merlot all over Maggie's new carpet!" He exclaims, still chuckling.

I feel the muscles in his bare shoulders rippling as he carries me upstairs to the bathroom and places me in the shower.

"I think you need to wash that out of your hair. Red wine really doesn't go with the blond."

He reaches behind me removing my bra before kneeling and sliding down my skirt, then my underwear. He briefly cups my ass with his hands and his tongue flicks across my clit before he rises. He kisses the top of my head softly.

"I'll meet you on the balcony downstairs in 20 minutes."

A few minutes later I step out onto the balcony shivering at the biting wind on my damp skin, my long, wet hair the only protection from the cold. The cold teak shakes slightly as someone steps outside. His warm bare arms encircle my waist.

"What took you so long?" I whisper, inhaling his scent and leaning my head back against his hard chest.

"I feel like I've been waiting for hours."

Lips find my neck, licking and kissing my cold skin. Hands slide across my stomach, finding and cupping my breasts.

"Years," he murmurs back.

I can feel him hard against my ass. I bend forward slightly pressing it harder against me. His fingers drift lower—right where I've imagined them for so many years.

"God, you're so wet," he moans as his fingers slide easily inside me.

"I've been dreaming of this day for so long."

He rubs my clit softly with his thumb, moving so I can feel the head of his cock between my legs, about to slide into my pussy. I open my eyes and gaze out across the expanse of forest that was the backyard. I only have a moment to think how perfect it all is when I hear an unearthly scream from behind me!

Jason pulls hastily away from me, shielding my nakedness from view.

Oh God, his wife.

My best friend.

Maggie.

I begin to stammer out an apology, until I can get to my clothes and run away.

I start to move around Jason and see the Chinese food that Maggie had so thoughtfully gone to get to cheer me up, spilled all over the floor where she had dropped it.

Maggie walks toward me. What I had taken for hysterical tears at catching her husband with her best friend was, in fact, laughter.

She leisurely removes her top to reveal large beautiful breasts, her nipples already hard. By the time she reaches us she has completely disrobed, bare skin gleaming with a thin sheen of sweat despite the chill of the air.

"It worked!" she chirps excitedly, throwing her arms around her husband.

I watch in shock as they begin kissing.

They part, Jason reaches out and takes my hand, leading me back inside the house and up the stairs to their expansive bedroom, Maggie following behind.

"Hold on!" I exclaim in shock.

Jason sits me on the edge of the bed and begins to nuzzle the bare skin on my thighs.

"What's going on? Is this some kind of joke?"

Maggie sits down next to me, her hand on my leg next to her husband's face.

"I've had a crush on you for years," she confesses.

"We've wanted to get you in bed with us for so long."

She begins to trail her fingertips up and down the inside of my thighs. I can feel my breath quickening in response to her touch.

"What do you think? Pretty please?"

Her beautiful dark eyes are connected with mine and I know what I want, what I've always wanted. I reach over and rest my hand on the back of her head, pulling her to me. Our lips meet and it is like nothing I've ever experienced before.

The bed shifts slightly as Jason climbs up next to us. He grabs me around the waist, spinning me away from her and to him. He pulls me on top of him and suddenly I'm in control.

I take a moment to admire his taught body under mine, as I quickly slither downward, sliding my hard body along his. I softly kiss the tip of Jason's hard cock before slipping it slowly into my mouth. He moans as I slowly slide him in and out of my mouth, my tongue flicking gently over the tip. He entwines his hands in my hair, pulling gently as I feel a small tongue parting the lips of my pussy. Maggie nibbles and sucks exactly where I want her to. She seems to knows my body as well as I do; her small fingers sliding inside me, gently stroking and caressing in all the right places.

I suck Jason harder and harder, spurned on by my own rapidly approaching orgasm. He thrusts his hips upward, grinding into my face. My breathing becomes ragged as I explode on my best friend's face, covering her in my juices. I lift my mouth from Jason to cry out just as he climaxes, spraying all over my chest. Leaning in to take him back into my mouth, I lick the last of his cum off him and suck him dry. I fall back onto the bed exhausted. Just as quickly, he is over me again, his tongue licking my face and chest clean.

Maggie sits down next to me, watching her husband, her face glistening. When he's done with me she throws him onto his back. She climbs on top of him, grinding her hips down on him as she moans in frustration.

I rise to my knees and begin licking where their bodies meet. My tongue twirls around his growing member and flicks her clit. She leans backward allowing me greater access. As I slide my tongue inside of her, my nose nuzzles her clit gently. She rises up and I can feel his cock hard and eager against my cheek. I grab it, guiding it gently into his wife's dripping slit. She cries out in ecstasy, sliding him all the way in.

I lower my mouth back to her pussy, dragging my tongue along the place where they're joined. It's only a second before I feel him begin to tremble, and they both burst simultaneously, soaking my face.

We all collapse together in a sweaty pile, silent other than our gasping, ragged breaths.

I reach out to my best friend and take her hand.

"I love you, and I think I always have."

I wait anxiously to hear what she will say, but she remains silent. After a moment she rolls over and takes me in her arms, brushing a kiss gently across my temple. I feel Jason take us both into his arms.

"We love you, too."

Jason holds us tight and, as I drift off to sleep, I know this is exactly where I belong.

Amanda is a new Goddess who joined Athena's in 2010. She loves every minute of it! Her positive attitude is a huge asset in educating people about their own bodies and sexuality. She is the loving mother of two beautiful boys, and an outstanding wife.

All the Discomfort of Home

By Goddess Maggie Russell

I had been hot and sticky all day, and had hoped that a cool, "playful" shower would refresh me and leave me feeling less irritated by my long day at work.

The shower hadn't worked.

Instead, I was now more frustrated because I hadn't even been able to play away some of my stress. I had tried, but the more I focused on my orgasm, the more it eluded me.

Finally, I threw in the towel, succumbed to being hot and bothered for the rest of the day, and crawled into bed, hoping that the fan moving air over my naked body would at least bring some relief.

When I awoke some time later, I saw that I had fallen asleep for a few hours, and the room was quite dark. As I stretched, preparing to get out of bed to see if John was home, I realized that something was not right. I couldn't move, my hands and feet were bound to the bed.

I started to cry out, but a large hand covered my mouth.

"Do not scream," he said.

"You will love every touch on your body, but do not make me mad, or I will have to take it out on you. Do you understand?"

I nodded. He removed his hand from my mouth and traced his fingers down my neck, between my breasts, and lower to the very top of the triangle of hair between my legs.

"I do love a good pussy," he said stroking me lightly. "And from the way yours is dripping already it will definitely be mine tonight."

I was torn. His touch was so light, so gentle, so pleasing, but in the pitch black room, I wasn't sure if this was John or not. He never spoke to me like this—he would never tie me up even though I'd begged him to.

I was sure I should be resisting this more, but my body and my desire for release won over the rational part of my brain, and I felt myself moving as much as I could, hoping to get those fingers inside me.

But as soon as I moved, he pulled his hand away.

"Begging for it already?" he laughed. "Well, this will be easier than I thought."

I waited what seemed like an eternity, but finally his hands returned, cupping my breasts, kneading them, pulling my nipples. As he focused all his attention on my breasts, I arched to meet his touch, my pussy tingling with anticipation of being handled next. But he took his time. Never had a man spent so much time stroking me like this.

Suddenly, I felt his tongue tracing circles around one nipple. He slowly sucked first one, then the other into his mouth. He continued kissing my body as he moved from my breasts, down my stomach. His hands skimmed the length of my torso, finally coming to rest between my legs.

"Please," I begged. "Please touch me."

"What did I tell you?" He chuckled into my stomach. "Easy."

His fingers continued their dance along my legs, caressing my feet, and coming back to the warm, wet spot between my legs. His finger slid between my pussy lips, then pulled back, teasing me even more. I tried desperately to force myself closer to his hands, desperate to have him buried deep inside me, but he moved away again.

Then, with a long stroke, his tongue finally caressed me, circling, then sucking on my clit. I groaned as he lavished attention on my swollen bud, still aching to feel him inside me.

He began stroking the entrance to my hole, making me cry out for more. Twisting against my restraints, I bucked against him, praying that he would enter me—that he would fill me up. He thrust his fingers deep inside me, and they continued working in tandem with his tongue, bringing me to one orgasm after another.

As I was about to reach my third, he stopped and removed himself from my pussy completely.

"No," I whimpered. "Please don't leave me, I need to feel you."

"Tell me how much," he demanded. "Tell me you want my cock."

"I want you so bad!" I cried. "Please give me your cock; please put it in my pussy."

"If I give you my cock," he warned, "You'll never want another man again."

"Please, please just give it to me."

I begged, tears threatening to pour down my cheeks.

Then, at last, he was deep inside me, so thick and hard that I felt like he was going to break me apart.

"Whose pussy is it?" He asked. "Is it mine?"

"God, yes!" I screamed. "No one's but yours!"

"Good," he replied, as he began to move within me.

I struggled against my restraints, wanting desperately to touch him, to pull him in deeper. He grabbed my hips, lifting me up off the bed as much as he could, angling himself to fit inside me even more. I thrust against him, feeling myself getting closer, and closer to another orgasm.

"Touch me." I pleaded. "Please touch me."

His hand found my clit again, flicking it, rubbing it in time with his thrusting inside me. His hands were everywhere, on my breasts, my arms, my belly. I screamed as I hit that highest peak of the strongest orgasm I'd had in a long time, and as he shuddered within me reaching his own orgasm, I finally felt relaxed.

A Goddess since 2009, Maggie's greatest joy in life is helping others. When not educating the world about sex and pleasure, Maggie enjoys spending time with her friends and family, singing, and of course, writing.

Lipstick

By Goddess Christine Reid

I know this will be worth it. I tried to convince myself, as the laces of my corset were tightened up the length of my spine. The Renaissance Fair was the one fall day my husband looked forward to every year— and the one I loathed! Don't get me wrong, I love the look of milky breasts heaved towards the heavens, barely containing ripe nipples that ached for air. I enjoyed wondering what, if anything, were under those kilts. But I could definitely do without the family atmosphere, the dust and the lack of proper bathrooms.

"This year will be the best one yet," my husband tried to convince me, as if he heard my unspoken thoughts. "You'll see."

He wrapped his hands around my cinched waist, and slowly began nibbling on my neck. His hands crept up as his mouth slowly drifted lower.

"One more thing to make this outfit complete." He turned away to grab a black jeweler's box that had been sitting on the dresser.

The box was larger than one that would hold a ring, and my eyes lit up at the thought of a large bejeweled necklace to drape over my neck, tickling the crevice my corseted breasts displayed.

Ceremoniously he opened the box.

"For you, my lady, or should I call you my wench?" he winked.

It was the most beautiful silver piece I had ever seen, but it definitely was not for my neck.

"Wear this while we're out today, to remind you of what's to come," he told me, gazing into my eyes with a devilish smile.

"Turn around," he commanded, as he lubed up this gorgeous Pure® plug.

He began kissing me at the base of my neck, one hand grabbing greedily at my chest along the way. He snaked his hands under my skirt, parting the path that his head would take. I felt teeth on my hips, and slowly my thong was trailing down towards my ankles.

The kisses continued up the back of my leg, lingering behind my knees, winding between my thighs. I could feel his warm mouth brush against my pussy lips, gently parting them with his tongue, lightly flicking my clitoris, then slow wet strokes through the depths of my canyon. His oral journey ended at my back door, where he circled my doorbell before pressing it.

Once, twice, a third time he buzzed, his burning breath huffing, waiting for access. Then cold, wet steel pressed its way in, my rear entry sucking in the bulbous plug.

I shivered and sighed as he patted my bum.

"Behave yourself today, and I promise to give you what you want when we get home," he bargained, as he turned to head to the car.

What I want? Since discovering this utterly taboo act, I simply could not get enough. His cock nestled tightly in my ass was what I wanted—NOW! I could not wait for this day to be over.

We ventured to the fairgrounds, a group of about thirty of us. As usual, my first stop was to visit my favorite wench, who would graciously keep the sweet honey mead flowing in my cup. This was the only thing that could get me through these visits.

The crowd moved towards the field, as the King had summoned everyone over to watch the main event—the joust.

Not one to follow rules, this was my time to fill up on more of my nectar, and I desperately needed some more. I offered "my Lord" a refill on his ale, he gave me a wicked smile and warned me that the King would not be happy if I left.

While walking away, I heard a great cheer. I turned to see that the King had just entered the field.

In the second floor window of a nearby barn, I saw a knave looking out, with a curious look on his face. It was not the look of a man cheering, but—it couldn't be—a look of pleasure? Honestly, who enjoys these ridiculous events?

I backpedaled into a great oak tree. I couldn't take my eyes off of this knave. I slowly hid behind the tree, hoping not to be noticed. From below the windowsill, gorgeous blond wavy locks bearing a flower crown appeared, and I realized I was watching the best show here.

She stood and bent over at the waist, her hair falling on top of her amazing, floating breasts, hands on the windowsill. As the horses galloped around the field, the knave kept rhythm, thrusting himself into the maiden.

I knew I shouldn't watch, but I couldn't help myself. Wrestling with the layers of my skirts, feeling that plug up my ass, and thankful for the privacy the tree provided, I could not keep from touching myself. All of these people watching the main event, and I have my own to watch. My mound could not get enough attention as it throbbed with excitement. The faster he pounded her, the faster I stroked between my lips, and still, I wanted more.

Excited by my view, and caught up in my own activity, I lost track of where I was.

Suddenly, everything went black, and I felt a hand on mine.

"The King does not like to be disobeyed," a gruff voice angrily breathed in my ear.

His big, calloused hand pressed mine deeper into my pussy, and I felt my knees give out.

On the ground, tightly blindfolded, I was helpless. I screamed but it was drowned by the raucous voices at the field. I was carried briefly, and dumped, with my stomach across…his lap?

I begged, I pleaded.

"Please let me go! My husband sent me to get some ale. I just got sidetracked! He'll be looking for me."

All I got in response was a slight chuckle, and the feeling of my skirts being lifted.

"Huzzah" echoed all around me. Were they watching me? Just as the first crash of the lance dove into an opponent's shield, I felt that meaty hand sting my exposed bottom.

"That is for disobeying the King."

Cheers erupted.

Crash. Smack.

"That is for your naughty display," he said.

I could feel the burning handprints, one on each cheek.

Crash. Smack.

"That is for being foolish enough to get caught."

Tears of humiliation streamed down my face, as tears of desire were welling in my cunt.

Crash. Smack. The hardest one yet.

"And that, maiden, is for enjoying this too much."

His hand did not raise for a fifth, but slid slowly down my burning red cheeks, discovering the hidden treasure my husband had buried earlier that morning. I imagined the steel gleaming in the sun, surrounded by bright red, swollen cheeks.

"Naughty, naughty wench. What's this?" he teased, turning the handle of my plug, reminding me of its presence.

Gently he tugged, and inadvertently, I tugged back, feeling that bulb gliding in and out.

Lower he wandered, one finger…two…slid inside me, his thumb wildly strumming my clit.

He was stroking my pussy, inside and out, with a deep, fluttering motion. I could hear the clapping, the screams and the movements. As the audience reaction got louder and louder, I could no longer contain myself. I sunk my teeth into his bare thigh and let out a scream of relief, spraying my own sweet mead over this punisher's hand.

"Tell me what you think they are doing—the knave and his beautiful fairy up in the barn," he demanded.

"He…they…" I sputtered, ecstasy still rippling through my body.

He wove his fingers through my hair, swiftly picked me up and pressed my stomach into the tree.

"Tell me now. What are they doing."

The rough bark was scraping against my hoisted tits, his bark-like hands grabbing at my hips.

"He's fucking her," I gasped. "He's fucking her from behind, while the King is watching, while I'm watching, and no one else knows."

I wrapped my arms around the trunk of the tree, drawing its strength to help me stand.

My body swallowed his trunk, in one easy movement, as he began acting out my very words.

I was terrified, elated, ashamed, free; each feeling rotated as he entered me roughly.

"He's...he's pulling her hair like the reins of the horse, he's telling her how lucky she is to be the blessed fairy who rides his cock."

"Lucky, yes..." he mused, tightening his grip on my own reins.

One hand was in my hair, holding my face back towards his, his other hand drifted down my backside, and began fiddling with my own lucky charm.

As the crowd died down, and the King spoke up, the thrusting suddenly stopped. My head was jerked back as his ale breath wrapped around my neck.

"Do you know what a real man wears under his kilt?" he asked.

I dropped to my knees, lifting this hem of his kilt, and was not surprised when I felt nothing but his own lance, attempting to part my lips. I desperately inhaled that cock in one motion, breathing his head into the back of my throat.

As the cheers erupted once more, he did as well, that delicious warm liquid slipped over my tongue.

I could hear the crowd moving. They were heading our way, and just like that, he was gone. I scrambled to my feet, untying the blindfold as quickly as I could. I saw my husband just a few feet away.

"You missed the show, and where is my ale?" he questioned.

Smiling, he added, "Best year yet?"

The sun was blinding and my head was swimming. I could not find words as I stared in his eyes. It was the best year yet, but how could I possibly begin explaining to him why this was the best. Being publicly punished and fucked by a stranger might make a good explanation, but not to my unassuming husband!

He gave a wicked smile as he simply muttered the word "Lipstick."

"What?" I asked, touching my lips—have I given myself away?

Bewildered, I stared at this husband of mine, as he raised his hand to my swollen lips.

Someone clapped him on the back. "Good show, kind sir. Same time next year?"

"Of course," he responds to the smiling knave and his fairy. "Good show," he echoed in agreement.

He turned to me and kissed my neck, licking down to my cleavage, grabbing my butt to ensure I was still plugged. That throbbing began all over again.

"Lipstick. It's what a real man wears underneath his kilt."

He smiled, ear to ear, as we joined the masses exiting the fairground. Best year yet.

Christine became a Goddess in 2007 to help women love sex as much as she does. She is grateful for her amazing Goddess friends and having her story published. She enjoys writing and cooking, and is lucky to be married to her fantasy man.

About
Athena's Home Novelties

Athena's is the dream of Jennifer Jolicoeur. After five years in the adult novelty in-home party plan industry as a distributor, she decided to create her own company —one that worked as a family unit with its distributors—a company based upon a distinctive sisterhood. Thus, Athena's Home Novelties was born.

Incorporated in 1998, and based in Woonsocket, RI, Athena's is one of the country's premier adult novelty party plan companies with over 1,500 active Goddesses operating in 39 states across the country.

Athena's Home Novelties is a member of the Direct Selling Women's Alliance (DSWA) and the Northern Rhode Island Chamber of Commerce (NRICC).

Our Mission: To empower women down the path of sexual education in the safe, comfortable environment of their own homes by offering only the highest quality products presented by a trained Athena's Goddess.

On the following pages, you will find information on the products mentioned in the stories included in this book.

To order any of these products, and more, you can go to our website at www.athenashn.com. You can also locate an Athena's Goddess near you who can help you host an Athena's party in the privacy of your own home.

Become a Goddess

Athena's Home Novelties is one of the country's leading at-home adult novelty companies. Our distributors (or Goddesses, as we like to call them) carry our message of self-love and relationship enhancement to thousands of customers each year.

Our product line includes something for everyone—young or old, female or male—and we carry only the highest quality products available.

Athena's offers two business plans, so you can choose the one that's right for you. Our Independent Goddess Plan allows you to purchase products at up to a 50% buying discount and pay yourself the night of the party. Our Freedom Goddess Plan allows you to do the party, submit it online to the home office, and we will handle the rest. Our Freedom Goddesses earn between 35% and 40% of their party sales.

To find out more, go to www.athenashn.com and click on "Become a Goddess" or call 877-ATHENAS!

The Celebrator®

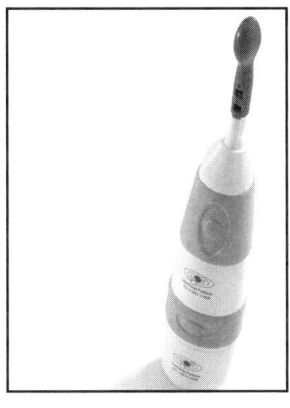

Athena's loves this fun gadget! It really was the talk of our headquarters during the testing period! To say it is effective to bring a woman to orgasm is an understatement! This unique gyrator is used externally to stimulate the key feminine "pleasure zones" found around the clitoris. Those of us who have used the Celebrator agree that it's the fastest, most intense orgasm we've ever had (and we've had many!). It looks like a toothbrush with a bulbous tip! On low you will experience 4,600 oscillations per minute. When you turn it up, you'll feel 9,600 oscillations per minute! This is a sex toy that will blow you away. Two AA batteries included.

AMAZING. Long, intense, orgasms. It took a little practice but as soon as you realize how you like to use it you will be blown away! —Sarah

Oh. My. Goddess. This toy is a must have for every woman with a clitoris! — Shannon

My orgasm lasted so much longer with this toy! — JPP

Instant orgasm—WOW! Much better than a vibrator. Oscillated me to ecstasy. —LeeAnn

This is it girls!! Just when you almost forgot what multiple orgasms were all about…hold on!! —Robi

This is the best toy I have ever bought. My husband and I have had a good time with it. I highly suggest you try this. So worth the money. The name really says it all! —Zamil

Coochy Shave Crème® (16 oz. pump)

A rash-free shave cream that's gentle enough for the most sensitive areas of your body, and can prevent those unsightly red bumps! Also highly recommended as a hair conditioner. Great on natural curls, and essential for the summer! Now available in a 16 oz. pump for easy dispensing in the shower.

This really works! I love it! I shared this product with all my friends and now they are also purchasing Coochy Crème. —Britt

My husband loved this product. He used mine all up shaving his head. He really liked the fact it wasn't too girly smelling. —Carmen

AMAZING! Every man and woman should have this product in their shower! It lasts forever and it works so well! —Jen

This is THE BEST product EVER! I shave with it and my skin is silky smooth. I condition my hair with it and it is like silk! Now my husband and kids use it too! Plus it makes a great lotion and removes eye makeup in a pinch! WOW! —Shelly

LOVE IT! It's so hard for me to shave my legs, underarms and pubic area because my skin gets so dry, but this is the best and only product I use now. My boyfriend uses it for his face (he feels so nice after). —Margaret

Seriously worth the money! This shave crème is great. I love it so much, I ONLY use it for its namesake, and never use anything else in that sensitive area. You will not regret giving this product a try! —Michelle

Crystal Chic G®

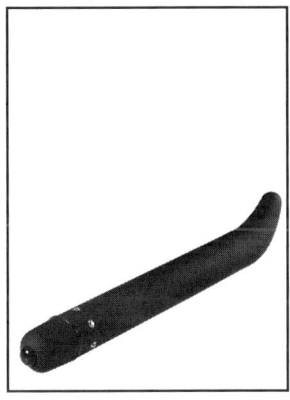

This tasteful vibe is finely dressed with genuine high quality crystals! Super slim design and sophisticated look appeals to women looking for a discreet plaything. Massage, tantalize and tickle your body in the shower, tub or bedroom. The three vibration speeds, silky smooth shaft and advanced electronic motor make for a pleasurable experience!

I absolutely love this! It has a smooth texture and the three speeds are amazing. Very quiet too! —Kim

I am a first time user and I was told by the Goddess to get this as a starter and wow! It was an amazing experience. —Melinda

Love Cuffs® (Black)

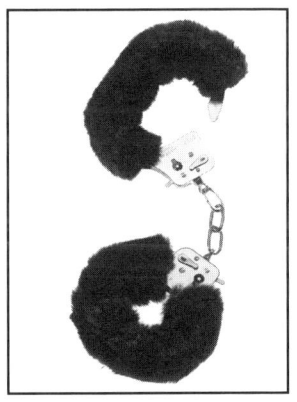

Safely explore your sexual imagination by surrendering yourself to your partner. These comfortable, adjustable faux-fur-lined handcuffs were created with the sensible submissive in mind. Keys included.

If you want to play 'cops and robbers' with your lover these are a great tool! No chafing as the fur is so soft! Perfect for roleplaying! —A bad girl

155

Massage & Body Oil®

Experience the "slip" of a professional service massage oil with the skin-rejuvenating properties that come from hemp and grape seed oils. Simply put, it is perfect for the massage enthusiast and is great for the recipient's skin. You won't want to wash it off!

This oil is amazing. My boyfriend has extremely sensitive skin and this product not only hydrates his skin but it also helps to eliminate red itchy blotches from the heat. It never hurts that its a great reason for me to have to "rub him down" either! —Dawnell

PETALS®

This beautifully detailed stimulator is designed for hands-free pleasure. Powered by a removable waterproof, multi-speed bullet, this delicate flower can join you in the tub or shower. The 3" insertable stamen emerges from the flexible petals to make your orgasms bloom. The nodules on the head are perfect for clitoral stimulation, too.

This is the first vibrator I ever owned and I LOVE it. The nubbies at the top and the petals both make great clit ticklers and the length is just right. —veryhappylady

Njoy Pure Plug® 1"

Equally fun for hot bedroom play or to wear all day for some naughty, discreet stimulation, Njoy's stainless steel Pure Plug truly shines where the sun does not. The Pure Plug combines a bulbous head for that delicious stretch of penetration, with a tapered stem for easy retention and long-term comfort. The handle is also very comfortable between the cheeks. The heavy steel adds a sense of fullness that will remind you of just how sensitive you really are "back there." You'll find this plug silky smooth and lube friendly. (2.25"x1" - 5oz.)

A dab of lube and it slides right in, a good way to prep for a night of anal, can keep it in for a little while as it sits quietly and discreetly between the butt cheeks. —J

Can't leave home without it. It's so comfortable and makes me feel naughty all day long. It heats up the workday —Vick

I absolutely love the feeling of this. —Dave

Under the Bed Restraint System®

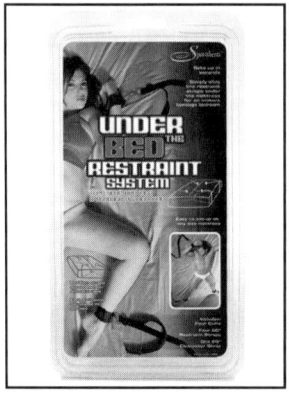

Turn any size bed into a place of binding pleasure! Restraint straps quickly fit beneath mattress or frame without hooks. Restrain your partner's arms or legs from the sides or the top and bottom of the bed. Portable and travel-sized. Includes four cuffs and restraint straps.

This is so much fun! We keep this under our mattress all the time. We just tuck the straps under the mattress and no one knows, and that way it's ready whenever we feel kinky! We love it! —Christy

Discreet and really comfortable to use! —Jo

A playground in a box. What a fun surprise to play helpless or take control. Very easy to hide from the snooping relatives. —KPM

I love this. My husband and I have so much fun with it. It's comfortable and easily adjustable. I recommend this to everyone who wants to get into the bondage play. —Lily

WET Light® 10.1 oz.

The world's leading lubricant! Water-soluble, non-staining, non-sticky. It has no odor or taste. Wet Light replenishes vaginal lubrication and aids in relieving vaginal dryness. Condom compatible. This formula does not contain Nonoxynol 9.

I like how easy it is to clean up! It only takes a few drops and lasts a long time. —I

GREAT! Just need a little bit, and it lasts. Easy clean up too. Love it!
—Barbi

WET Platinum® 3.1 oz.

This premium formula is made of 100% pure silicone. It stays slick longer than any water-based formula. Latex friendly, it's perfect for anal sex and underwater play. Not recommended for frequent internal vaginal use.

Absolute best product to use for anal sex! Highly recommended!
—Kristie